THE BLOOD OF KANTA

THE WOLVES OF KANTA SERIES: BOOK 2

MARLENA FRANK

EB ISBN: 978-1-955854-06-1
PB ISBN: 978-1-955854-07-8
HB ISBN: 978-1-955854-08-5

To Mom and Dad,
For believing in me when I didn't believe in myself.
Thank you for your support in everything I do and for inspiring me
to pursue my passion.

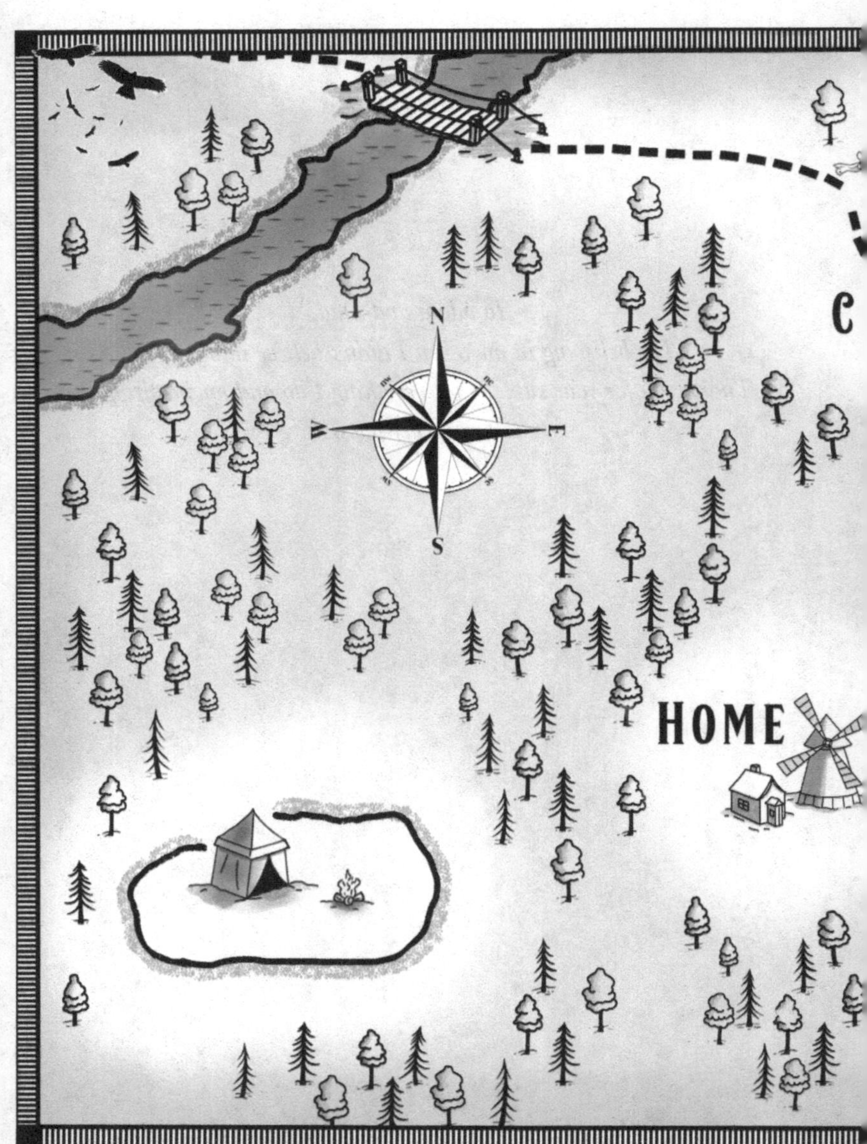

N
S
E
W
HOME
C

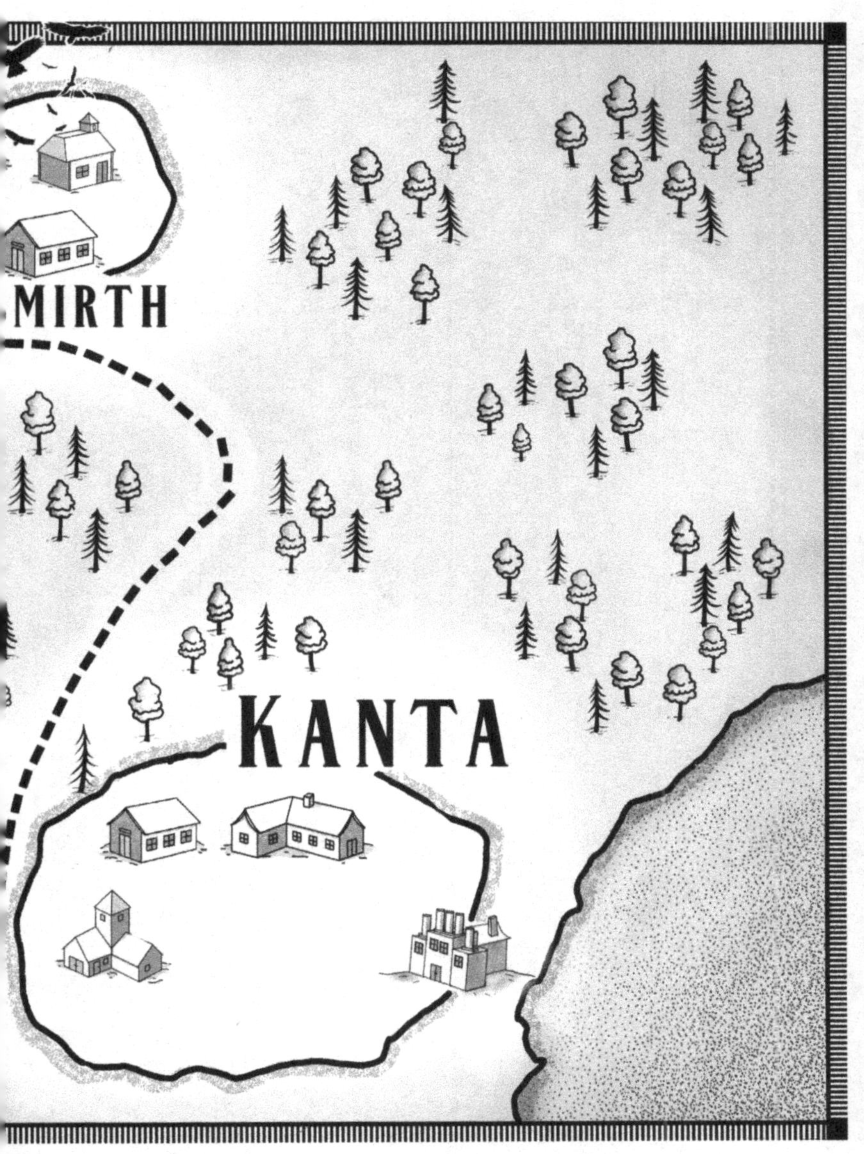

MIRTH
KANTA

PART 1

The Hunter

1

A WEAK STOMACH

THE BLOOD WAS TERRIBLE.

There was just so much of it, and Mercy couldn't bring herself to look at the severed limbs that had been dragged away. There wasn't much left of Carter, but he was still awake and still aware. Thomas had given her the task of dragging his mutilated body to one of the werewolf cages, so Mercy grabbed him from beneath the stubs of his arms, and set about her work. All the while, he pleaded and begged.

"Death would be better," he groaned into her ear through bloodied, trembling lips. His breath still smelled of cheap ale and Mercy scrunched her nose as she dropped his shaking body onto the floor of the cage, which reverberated with a metallic thump.

He begged her for help, but where was his compassion when he chased her through the woods? Where was his pity when he stalked her down to the laboratory and tried to shoot her? Yet now, he expected her to show him pity. Worse was that a part of her wanted to help him, and that only made her rage burn hotter.

"Be quiet," she snapped through clenched teeth. She felt the uncertainty in her words though, the hesitation in her actions. She didn't like it. He deserved his fate, deserved far worse for also killing her father, but still her hands shook. She closed and locked the cage before turning back to Thomas. She nearly tripped over Carter's ruined leg as she turned. Briefly she looked at it for the first time. It looked more like a ravaged carcass she might find in the woods rather than something that used to be a human limb. The deep teeth marks on it indicated how powerful the jaws were that had torn it free.

She shook herself. It didn't matter. He wouldn't be human for much longer anyway. So why couldn't she stop shaking?

"You're stronger than you look," Thomas said, forcing her gaze away from the limb. He stood near the wall with a crooked smile and one metallic hand over the bloody stump of his shoulder.

Mercy took a deep breath, gave a short nod in response, and turned away. To be honest, she felt terrible. Her stomach kept going tight whenever she thought about what was happening. Not to mention her injuries still hadn't fully healed. Her side ached endlessly, her legs shook, and her hands didn't want to obey.

She had only just barely recovered from tumbling down a cliffside, straining her back, injuring her side, and becoming ill. She was lucky not to have a bullet in her skull from Carter or to have been kidnapped by

Mitchell once she was able to walk. Thomas had released his werewolves into the laboratory before Carter shot his mechanical arm. If she hadn't removed it, they would both be dead.

Of course, if Carter hadn't tried to kill her, she would be the one locked in a werewolf cage getting bitten and transformed. Instead, Carter was taking her place as Thomas's latest experiment. She wasn't sure if she should feel horrified or grateful. She shuddered and felt a hand on her shoulder.

"Are you okay?" Thomas asked, his lazy eye slow to catch up to his good one.

"I'm okay," she lied, trying to slow her galloping heartbeat.

"Good, because I need you to fetch my research journal from my office." He gestured to a side door she hadn't noticed before, designed to blend in with the stone walls like the entrance to the lab. It was a normal door with a normal handle, unlike the giant metal one with the three big bars.

Thomas paced back and forth, his attention back on the cage. "You should find it on my desk. It should be easy to spot. Hurry though, night will be upon us soon!"

She stepped in, glad to put some distance between her and Carter's cries. The room was a mess. Mercy's father would have never let her keep a space like this in their house. A worn, red armchair sat in a corner that looked as old as she was. Stacks of glass vials and beakers sat on the shelves beside bowls of darts tipped with needles, similar to the ones she used to make for her father.

What took up most of the room were the stacks of papers. They filled every corner, every crevice, and every space where they could be shoved. Some were covered in handwritten notes and sketched diagrams. Others looked like important letters complete with official stamps. Then her eyes fell on the tall pair of bookshelves beside a massive flat desk.

Mercy's jaw dropped. She had never seen so many books in her life. Father had only owned five and they were falling apart. Many nights she stitched the pages back into the threadbare spines. These books were leather-bound, she knew, because she could smell the oils. What she assumed was Thomas's research journal was splayed out and easy to find on the desk, complete with a pen and a refillable inkwell. Instead of reaching for that, she was drawn to the books. She put a hand out, fingers inches away from a smooth, ribbed leather spine titled *The Nature of Matter and Change*. She had almost touched the engraved, golden letters when a scream echoed from the laboratory.

She jumped back as though her fingers had been burned.

"Hurry up, child. The transformation has already begun!" Thomas called urgently from the next room.

Mercy chided herself for getting distracted and grabbed the research journal and pen before bolting for the door.

Thomas gestured eagerly for the materials. Once she approached, he sat down on the metal floor and urged her to put the tools down on the ground. "Excellent! Thank you, Mercy!" He flipped to a blank page, took the pen cap off with his teeth, and spat it to the floor. "A full transformation from start to finish! How glorious!"

Glorious was hardly the word Mercy would have used for it. Carter's face, one of the only places that hadn't been ravaged by the werewolves, was covered in sweat. His eyes were unbearably wide and his jaw was clenched so hard Mercy was afraid he might bust out his teeth. Despite how torn up his arms and legs looked, his muscles were rigid as spasms rolled through him. Each one made him lose even more blood from his wounds. He already lay in a puddle of it. Mercy put a hand to her throat, hearing her own pulse pounding in her ears, as she watched the blood pour out of Carter.

The man's eyes dilated and all his muscles relaxed. A tear fell down one of his cheeks. He looked Mercy in the eye and croaked out in a hoarse voice, "Please kill me."

A cold shiver crept down her spine and she crossed her arms over her chest, slowly backing away from the cage. Thomas sat on the floor beside her, scribbling away with a rapid intensity while humming a tune to himself. He didn't seem to hear the pleas at all. Either that or he was purposefully ignoring them.

One of Carter's bones gave a loud, wet snap and he screamed. Mercy jumped and instinctively put her hands over her ears as another bone snapped and reshaped itself. When he rolled over onto his stomach, she could see that his back was ripped down the center, exposing his spine, which protruded out and snapped as it lengthened and reshaped.

"I'm sorry." Mercy backed away, knowing well that Thomas couldn't possibly hear her over the screams, but unable to bring herself to stay any longer. Carter's screams went to a higher, more terrible pitch as his body morphed ever further away from human. "I'm sorry, Mr. Farrell," she muttered again, barely finding the breath for words. "I have to go."

He nodded a couple of times but didn't look up as she fled, careful to step around the bloodied mess that Carter had left pooled in the middle of the floor. Out of the laboratory, she walked up the inclined passage quickly, trying to put as much distance as possible between her and Carter's cries. The scent of lamp oil pulled at her, pushing away the powerful scent of brimstone down below. She kept her eyes on her feet, focusing on making each footstep land and not to pitch to the floor. She thought she might pass out, with the way the stars swirled around her vision and how her head felt like it was floating.

At last, she stepped out into the stairwell, away from the shadow of the laboratory entrance and ran to the steps. She put her hands on the stairwell railing and looked up at the metal spiral stairs that climbed upwards. Closing her eyes, she took a deep breath. The air out here was hot and heavy from the ever churning grinders. She could hear them turning, and for some reason it calmed her. She could still hear Carter's screams but they were more muted, more distant.

In the corner of the room lay the remains of Mitchell and Mercy averted her eyes. She couldn't handle seeing more blood and just spotting the body of the man who had just tried to kill her splayed across the metal floor made her stomach turn.

She took one deep breath, then another. As long as she didn't look at Mitchell, she could think out here. She didn't feel trapped like she had down in the laboratory. What had happened to her? She hated Carter. If Thomas hadn't gotten the werewolves to bite him, it would be her down there instead, screaming in pain from her bones breaking and reshaping, tendons snapping and reconnecting, and with a mind slowly devolving into something monstrous. But if Carter had his way, she would be dead in the woods, eaten alive by ravenous werewolves. He deserved every ounce of pain he received. So why was she trembling from head to toe? Why had she almost passed out back there?

Black paint flecked off in her fingers from the banister she gripped, but the railing kept her steady and grounded. She was scared, she realized, but that didn't explain everything. She had known what she was getting into by accepting the risk of being turned into a werewolf. She had known that it was a terrible fate to give to anyone, even Carter, but she had never seen it happen before. She had known it had to be a terrible process, but seeing Carter's torture made it more real. Hardly anyone had seen a werewolf transform. Not even her father had seen a transformation in his lifetime.

Something rattled the staircase from above and Mercy backed away. Had there been more potential kidnappers than just Carter and Mitchell? She thought back and wondered if they possibly had a third accomplice. There was honestly no telling. Mercy berated herself for stepping out without even a set of electric prongs as a weapon. That kind of forgetfulness had gotten her into this situation to begin with. She backed toward the laboratory entrance, trying to hear more than Carter's screams below and the grinders in the distance, but there was too much background noise. She tried to tell herself that it was just the metal settling, but her instincts told her otherwise.

Father used to say that instincts were sometimes all there was between life and death. What mattered was whether or not they were heeded. So Mercy turned around, intent on running down to the lab to get a weapon, but instead she nearly ran into Leyda.

"Leyda," Mercy whispered, looking her up and down. "You're alive."

The bandages around her face had fallen in her struggle with Mitchell and she had a dark, wet spot on her side. She was staring up toward the ceiling, breathing hard. Had she been up here the entire time and Mercy just hadn't noticed?

Leyda gave a sort of smile, her face contorting in all the wrong places. Before it had made Mercy shiver, but this time it didn't. Maybe she was just grateful to see a friendly face, or maybe she was still whirling from the horrors of Carter's transformation, but Mercy felt relief wash over her. She felt such a sudden surge of relief that she pulled Leyda into an awkward hug.

Leyda gasped in surprise, then held her breath for a moment. Finally, she whispered in a gravelly voice, "That's not necessary, child. Please release me."

Mercy pulled away with chagrin. "I'm sorry, I just—I thought you were dead."

Leyda put a finger to her lips. Then Mercy heard a

sound from above on the staircase. She glanced behind her toward the still chamber. This time she heard it clearly. It had not been her imagination. What was worse was she recognized the sound. She had heard it from the caged werewolf she and her father had brought to the mill before. She heard it again when she was down in the laboratory. It was the sound of werewolf claws scraping on metal. She broke out in a sweat.

Mercy turned to Leyda, but she appeared to be tracking something on one of the top levels of the stairwell. She tried to see what was up there, but she couldn't see anything beyond the staircase. She swallowed down the lump in her throat.

"It's okay," Leyda whispered, though her body language spoke otherwise.

Mercy stood frozen, listening to the werewolf claws scrape and the footfalls land softly on the metal landing. Finally, Leyda relaxed.

"Okay, that was strange," Leyda muttered.

"Why are werewolves wandering around the mill?" Mercy asked, panic filling her voice.

Leyda gave a low chuckle. "I could ask you that same question. They passed by me as I lay recovering by the door."

Slowly it dawned on Mercy what had happened. Thomas had released the werewolves from the laboratory and released them on Carter, but once they were finished, they had easy access to the rest of the mill. Suddenly every shadowed corner was suspect. She had seen what they had done to Carter. She had tripped over one of his limbs just a few minutes ago. She knew what carnage they were capable of, tame or not.

Leyda clasped her shoulder and gave her a shake. "Easy, child. They won't harm you."

Mercy glanced at her with questioning eyes, wondering if Leyda was delirious from blood loss.

"They didn't harm you before, did they? And they clearly didn't kill Carter, judging by his screams. Remember they have their minds, child. They can think like I can. Just because they are dangerous doesn't mean you're in danger."

Mercy shook her head. "That doesn't make any sense."

Leyda sighed and put a hand to her bloody side. Mercy's terror was momentarily forgotten.

"You need help! Should I send a message to Dr. Keene? Or—maybe Thomas would be better."

She shook her head. "No, I'm still beast enough to handle a measly lead bullet. This will be healed soon, but we probably ought to collect the werewolves before they start breaking things." She took a deep breath. "Come along, let's get this over with."

"But I don't have a weapon," Mercy stammered. "Not even a set of prongs!"

"You have a tongue, don't you?"

Mercy clenched her jaw. "You want me to ask them nicely to come downstairs?"

That prompted a full laugh from Leyda. "If you can't even wrangle a few tame werewolves, then you don't have the stomach for this place, child." She stepped around Mercy and started up the steps. "You might as well tell Thomas now, so he can figure out what to do with you. Though I assure you, very little in this town abides a weak stomach or a cowardly heart—the mill is no exception."

Mercy watched her take a few steps up the stairwell, leaning heavily on the railing. Everything within told her this was a very bad idea.

What Leyda didn't know was Mercy saved Thomas's life down in the laboratory by pulling off his mechanical arm. That might make her and Thomas even, or possibly he might owe her a life debt. Either way Mercy was fairly confident she could ask Thomas for help, and he would let her stay without having to wrangle were-wolves, but she knew she wouldn't be happy with that kind of privileged life.

Mercy had spent her entire life earning her keep at her father's house, and she had no intention of stopping. One lesson she had learned when she was very young: boredom was sometimes far worse than menial work. If she hoped to stay at the mill and earn her keep, she would need to start following Leyda's advice, even if it did seem crazy.

Mercy sighed and hurried to catch up to Leyda. "Come on, let me help you. I can't let you do this yourself."

Leyda's eyes hardened, "Kanta doesn't abide a kind heart either, child."

"Would you rather do this on your own then?" she asked.

Leyda pursed her lips and allowed Mercy to help her climb.

THE SHADOWS LENGTHENED as the sun sank lower beneath the horizon and Mercy was struck by how alien the tower felt with its dark metal and stone. Their footsteps up the stairs made the metal groan and creak, which unsettled her. The spiral staircase had many landings as it rose up the tower. There were many doors that Mercy did not know, and she could only speculate what was hidden behind each one. It was a bizarre place to live.

When they reached the correct floor, Mercy was surprised. She would have assumed that most of the werewolves would have left the tower or tried to leave the mill completely, but Leyda insisted the werewolves were there. Just a few floors up was her room, on a similar landing of riveted black metal flooring, metal walls, behind an ordinary wooden door. This door was ajar.

Mercy's pulse quickened and her stomach dropped at the sight of it, and she was unable to make her feet move. That familiar lightheadedness from before came again and she took a deep breath, not wanting to faint in front of Leyda. She knew she would never hear the end of it. Leyda would forever see her as weak, and despite what she might be capable of, the judgment would be cast.

To her surprise, Leyda didn't push her. Instead she let go of Mercy's hand and took the lead.

"Any of you in here?" Leyda pushed open the door and stepped inside. The hinges creaked in protest and

Mercy winced. If the werewolves had somehow missed their footsteps coming up the staircase, they certainly hadn't missed that. She had an inexplicable impulse to run forward and shut the door, but that wouldn't help anything. Leyda turned, scanned the room, then stood up straighter. Without saying anything to Mercy, she stepped out of view.

Mercy waited. What felt like ten minutes passed, though it was probably only a few seconds. She didn't hear or see anything, and not knowing what was happening out of sight was the worst. Had Leyda been attacked? Was she fighting for her life? She would never find out if she stayed rooted to the spot. She forced her legs to move as quietly as possible and approached the doorway. She entered the room sideways, avoiding touching the door to prevent it from creaking again. She didn't want to announce her presence. She controlled her breathing like she would on a hunt with her father, so she wouldn't attract the werewolf's attention.

As she stepped fully inside, it took a moment for her eyes to adjust to the darkness of the room. Very little light came in from the windows and none of the candles had been lit. A strong, tingling smell made her nose itch and she had to refrain from sneezing. It was the scent of spices, salted meats, and a freshly scrubbed floor. The kitchen.

She glanced to the back of the room and then spotted it: a large, silver werewolf crouched over a big chunk of beef jerky. She pinned down with both clawed hands and gnawed on it, tearing off long strips with her sharp teeth. She ate like a hungry dog and the fur around her neck and muzzle was covered in bits of the meat.

Clad all in black, Leyda was harder to spot, but when Mercy saw her, her jaw dropped. Leyda stood beside the silver wolf with her arms crossed and looked very annoyed. She wasn't even trying to keep her distance. Close enough that all the silver werewolf would have to do was lean to the side and sink her teeth into her. Sure, Leyda was part werewolf but she was so much smaller that Mercy had no doubts the werewolf could hurt her with hardly any effort.

"Come on, Angela, you and your daughter both know you aren't supposed to be in here," Leyda said.

Mercy blinked. *Both?* A smaller werewolf was there too, she realized, almost hidden by her mother. Mercy covered her mouth, suddenly aware how loudly she was breathing and remembering to follow her father's training. The silver werewolf, no, *Angela* tore off more strips, lapped them into her mouth with a long, pink tongue, and licked at her lips. She turned to Leyda, her expression seeming equally annoyed, then turned back to her dinner.

Leyda gave a heavy sigh before turning to Mercy. "Are you going to help, or do you plan to stare all night?"

Angela the werewolf gazed at Mercy, golden eyes glinting from the light of the stairwell through the open door. Mercy's legs turned to lead weights. Her stomach went tight and she held her breath, remembering that night out in the woods with her father. A werewolf's gaze could stop even the most well-trained hunter in their tracks, she remembered him saying, and once again she felt pinned in place by those amber eyes. An instant later, the anxious moment passed as the silver werewolf turned back to her meal again, clearly unimpressed.

Leyda snarled in Mercy's direction. "You're a big help."

Mercy looked at Leyda in outrage. She was a human. She couldn't help her natural reaction to them. However she also knew there was truth to Leyda's words. Thomas could sit and read a book to Leyda when she was fully transformed and he did not panic. Her father had trapped many werewolves and not been frozen in place by their gaze. Maybe Mercy *was* soft.

Leyda continued, "Maybe you would have been more useful transformed."

The words stung.

Mercy always tried to make herself useful at home. That was one of the reasons she wanted to be a werewolf hunter like her father. She hated feeling helpless and useless while her father did all the work. He caught the werewolves and he picked up supplies in town. She was never allowed to do any of it. She couldn't count the number of times she asked him to train her to be a hunter before he finally relented. She wanted to do more to help, to be more capable. Even now she froze up just because a werewolf looked at her.

Anger sparked that had been building beneath the surface for years. It wasn't aimed at her father or at a trapper like Mitchell or Carter, but at her predicament.

Once again she was in a place where she knew very little and felt like she had to run to catch up with anyone.

But unlike at home where she was rarely given the chance to learn, here she had the opportunity to prove herself. For the first time in her life she could learn and grow in ways she couldn't have dreamed at home. She refused to allow Leyda to intimidate her or draw her into complacency. This was her chance, maybe the only chance she would get. If she wanted to do more with her life, if she wanted to become greater, she needed to act.

"Come on you two," she said in a voice that was too quiet and timid.

She might as well be talking to a pair of fish for all the attention they gave her. Leyda watched her in silence. It was hard to figure out what she was thinking with the way the shadows fell on her partially bandaged face. Was she judging her? Waiting for her to do more? Father's training was like that. He would silently wait for her to follow a command or to make the right move, and if she didn't, she would regret it. His brand of training included trying to read his mind, an impossible task that meant she usually stepped out of line and got punished. It served to dissuade her from trying anything. Though in retrospect, maybe that was the true lesson he wanted to teach her from the beginning: to give up, to stop trying, to stay put and do whatever he asked her to do. She would be punished if she tried to escape him.

But her father was dead. He no longer had a say in what she did or what she thought. If she hoped to survive in this place, she needed to learn to step up and train herself.

Somehow Mercy found the strength to move her feet. She approached the table and stood across from the mutilated beef jerky. It might have smelled good before, but now it was covered in werewolf slobber, so it reeked of sulfur. She tried again.

"I need you two to go back to your cells. Please."

Angela, the silver werewolf, barely glanced up at her, and instead bared her teeth as she bit into the meat. Mercy winced. Leyda didn't say a word. Fine, she would try again.

"I know you don't want to and I don't blame you. But I need to find the others, and I can't do that until you both go back. You two might not be getting into any trouble, but they might be. I don't want any of you to get hurt."

That got her attention. Angela looked up from her meat, her long pink tongue lapping at her lips. Her jaw was strong enough to take off Mercy's hand in a single bite. She had seen werewolves bite through tree branches before without any trouble. Mercy felt a drop of sweat go down her back.

"Please," she said again, not backing down from Angela's gaze. The werewolf snorted then looked between her child and the salted meat strewn about the table. Mercy nodded, grasping what she meant. "You can bring it with you if you want."

That seemed to excite her and she leaned over to nudge the child who gave out a whine. The silver werewolf snapped at the air once and the child went silent. In one enormous hand that could have easily wrapped around Mercy's skull, she picked up her child's salted meat and her own. The little one started lapping at the table where the meat had been until the mother snapped her jaws again, this time including a low growl that made Mercy's pulse quicken. The child gave a final meek retort before pulling away from the table.

Angela led the way walking on three legs, and the little one followed behind. She turned back once to glare at Mercy. Mercy's legs trembled beneath her as the eyes landed on her, but she didn't collapse.

"Thank you," Mercy managed through a cracked voice.

Angela snorted before heading out with her child. It was only when Mercy heard the clicking of their claws on the steps and the squealing of the metal staircase as they descended that she finally relaxed. She had to lean against the table to keep from falling to the ground.

"Well, aren't you surprising." Leyda stepped carefully around the messy table.

Mercy gave a nervous little laugh. "Yeah, that surprised me, too."

Leyda put a hand on her shoulder. Mercy tried to stop her body from shaking, from betraying her terror to Leyda, but knew she couldn't.

"That was very brave for a human."

Mercy shook her head and gave another anxious laugh. She thought Leyda expected her to step forward. She thought she was disappointed. But Leyda wasn't her father, was she?

"No, I mean it, Mercy. I'm impressed." Leyda nodded.

Mercy gaped at her, at a loss for words for a long moment. Leyda seemed impossible to impress, but somehow she had. Pride swelled in her that she hadn't felt for quite some time.

She whispered, "Thank you."

Leyda released her and headed for the door. "Perhaps I judged you too quickly before. I apologize for that."

An apology too? Mercy gave another nervous laugh and felt her cheeks flush. She wasn't used to receiving praise for her actions.

"Come, there will be time later to collect yourself. I hope you're ready to do that stunt a few more times today." She hurried out of the room and started up the stairs.

Mercy leaned against the table and put her head back. Honestly she wasn't sure if she could do that again. She barely did it the first time. But if the other werewolves were as reasonable, maybe she had a chance. She glanced toward the door and heard Leyda reach the second landing. As injured as she had been before, Leyda seemed fine now. Werewolf healing really was fast. Mercy wished she could recover her own nerves so quickly.

Her legs shook as she pushed away from the table. She dreaded what was to come. It wasn't until she reached the kitchen door that she she gasped and realized what had happened.

Leyda had called her by her name. She had never

done that before. Even when she was trying to convince her to be bitten and turned into a werewolf, even when she found her in the woods, she had never said her name. Perhaps she really had impressed her, maybe even gained a small amount of respect.

Father had never been impressed with any of Mercy's work. The best feedback she could get from him was a lack of feedback. At the end she couldn't even lure in the right kind of werewolf. To have someone actually acknowledge that she did something right for once, someone she respected, was thrilling. Mercy hurried to catch up with Leyda, but instead she nearly tripped over the door frame. As excited as she was, her body still told her to slow down. She still had a lot to learn.

ROUNDING UP WEREWOLVES was a piece of cake compared to cleaning up Mitchell's body. Mercy had seen plenty of dead animals before, but it was different seeing a dead person, especially someone who had been trying to kidnap or kill her just a short while ago. Mercy's gaze kept drifting over to his lifeless eyes as she tried to clean the floor.

Leyda had given her the task, perhaps to see if she really did have the stomach for this work, and Mercy couldn't say no. How could she when she was determined to prove herself?

"Don't feel sorry for that one," Leyda told her in a cool voice as she leaned against the stairwell. She must have noticed Mercy's hesitation. "He deserved far worse than what I gave him." She leveled her with a heavy gaze. "He would have done far worse to you if he could have, and he certainly would have reveled in killing me."

Mercy dipped her mop into the bucket of water that had turned red, then flopped it back down on the metal floor. Despite how much she tried to focus on her task, her gaze kept slipping back to his mutilated body. At any moment she wondered if he might twitch awake or whisper her name. She swallowed down her fear and dragged the mop across the ground, even though it only seemed to spread the blood more than pick it up.

Mitchell had been a terrible person in life. He had worked for Thomas and been the mastermind behind killing her father and trying to kidnap Mercy for the human trafficking ring that ravaged the city of Kanta. Thomas explained that it wasn't the werewolves who were to blame for all the missing women, but the traffickers and judging by their methods, Kanta was lucky to have any women at all. Leyda spoke as if she had encountered people like him before. A question came to Mercy's lips before she could stop herself.

"You could have killed Thomas the day you ripped his arms off. Why didn't you?"

She glanced to Leyda who had fixed the wrappings on her face. It made it harder to read her expressions, but she did notice how her shoulders tensed and the deep breath she took. Clearly Mercy had hit some kind of nerve.

Her curiosity got the better of her. "You two were enemies at one point, weren't you? Thomas had you working a grinder. What makes Thomas different from

Mitchell? Why is he downstairs taking notes on Carter's transformation while Mitchell is…" She trailed off. She looked at his body again and all the words for how to describe it flew out of her head. It was like her mind censored itself at the mere mention of his body, like it couldn't even wrap itself around the concept.

Leyda lowered herself down to sit on the floor near the base of the stairs. She stared at Mitchell's body for a moment before shaking her head. "Mitchell was a fool. All he wanted was money. Thomas was different." She went quiet for a moment, lost in thought. Then she pointed to a corner. "Clean up that corner first, then I'll take his body downstairs. The furnace workers will take care of him."

Mercy imagined his body being thrown in with the fires that helped run the mill, his essence becoming part of the place she now called home. There was something terrifying about that. Instead of complaining, she pursed her lips and did as asked. She tried not to think about how many bodies they had to cremate like that. It seemed to be a common problem.

As she started mopping the corner, her side throbbed in protest. It had been a dull ache since she went down into the lab with Carter on her heels, and it had remained a dull pain. But the mopping aggravated it again. Each drag across the metal floor was met with a pulse of pain. When she finished, she put a hand to her side, remembering the exact tree limb that was responsible. She expected Leyda to say something chiding, but instead she was silent. Mercy glanced at her. Her eyes were glassy as she stared at the corpse.

"You asked me why I spared Thomas's life, but honestly, I'm not sure. I wanted to kill him. I wanted him dead with every fiber of my being." She let out a shaky breath. "I climbed those walls knowing I could have fallen to my death at any moment, but I didn't care. I only had eyes for him. Then I had him pinned beneath me. He was begging, pleading with me. I laughed in his face while the claws of my feet dug into the soft skin of his shoulders. That's what made me pause. There was shock in his eyes, not at me pinning him, but at my cackle into the sky. I think he knew in that moment that something was off about me. His skin was easy to tear apart. I barely had to apply much pressure when I took his arms."

Mercy shuddered at her words.

"He howled in pain, and I...I guess I felt bad for him. I realized that he and I weren't that different." She turned to Mercy with a scowl. "Then his guards came in with guns blazing and I thought: this is it, this is my end. It would have been an appropriate death for me. Not pretty, but appropriate. Then Thomas told them to stop. I thought he had passed out from the pain. I would have. I wondered if I should have killed him then, for I didn't know what punishment he had planned for me next."

Leyda got to her feet and a small, tinny sound echoed throughout the stairwell. Mercy jumped.

"What was that?"

Leyda leaned down to pick up a bullet off the floor. "Carter's attempt to kill me." She removed her headscarf. There wasn't much blood on the fabric, but there was a bloody mess on the side of Leyda's skull, matted in her hair and fur against her scalp. "The dimwit didn't even have the foresight to use a silver bullet." She felt the wound for a few minutes before securing the wrappings again.

The wood of the mop bit into Mercy's fingers as she clutched it in her hands. "That was in your skull?"

She nodded with a laugh that felt more menacing than humorous. "Yes, it was. It feels much better now, thank you for asking." She stretched before adding, "Your injury won't be so quick to heal. Here, let me get this dimwit out of here and you can leave the rest of this mess for me."

Mercy nodded and put her mop aside. "Thank you, I think mopping made it worse."

Leyda hefted Mitchell's body over her shoulder with ease. "I'll get this. You'll have to help down in the laboratory."

Mercy froze. "With Carter?"

Her eyes crinkled in a smile. "Clearly they're hungry if Angela and her young one were any indication. Ask Thomas how to feed them. He'll give you instructions."

Mercy reached for the mop. "I can take care of the mess instead. I don't mind!"

Leyda laughed as she headed for a wooden door opposite the laboratory. A chill went down Mercy's spine at the sound. "You'll be fine. Take some prongs with you if you must, but I don't recommend using them. You'll likely only anger them. Besides, you helped wrangle them. I think they like you."

"But where do I get food for them?"

Leyda turned back to her, one foot through the door. "Wasn't your father a werewolf hunter and you his small apprentice?"

She gave a feeble nod.

"Then I'm sure you'll be fine. You have trapping in your blood. I'm sure you'll be a natural at caring for caged werewolves."

At that moment Mercy understood that Leyda was mocking her. Before she could figure out a response, Leyda was through the door and gone.

She stood for a moment trying to figure out what to do. The mop leaned against one wall and a few sets of prongs on another. Leyda couldn't truly force her to go take care of werewolves. She had no hold over her now that Carter had taken her place and Mitchell was dead. Plus caring for werewolves sounded far too similar to caring for the household like she used to for her father. She went toward the mop.

Still, she had always wanted to be a werewolf hunter. Sometimes if the weather was too bad to get the truck through the woods, they would have to keep the caught werewolves at home and tend to them for days at a time. Her father would be disappointed in her if she chose to mop instead of tending to his prized beasts. But these weren't beasts, were they? They had their minds still, or at least had a good bit of their minds. They had seen her alongside Thomas and now Leyda, so they should see her as friendly. At least, that's what she hoped.

She was here to learn. She was here to grow, and that meant letting go of things that felt comfortable.

That meant grasping hold of uncomfortable tasks instead. She may have only helped capture one werewolf with her father, but she had helped him do the job for years. She built the needles, she prepared the cages, and she handled the things her father was too weary to deal with. She also helped care for those werewolves stuck at home for days within a cage. She might not have all the training to be a werewolf hunter, but she knew a little about caring for werewolves.

Glancing once more at the mop, she picked up the prongs instead, but she didn't do it for her father. She did it because she was tired of being helpless. She wanted change. She wanted the courage, and the strength, to take care of herself. Caring for a bunch of tame werewolves might be a low bar, but it was a start.

She stared up at the metal spiral staircase and breathed in the scent of the mill and its mechanical clouds of steam. Outside, the grinders continued to turn and Mercy turned toward the laboratory. She made a decision that would forever change her life.

2

UNDER THE SKIN

THE MILL REQUIRED more maintenance than Mercy ever expected. Slowly she did gain more of a stomach for the gruesome tasks she was given. She helped clean the walls of the grinders and monitored newly acquired werewolf workers. Whenever she could, she offered to help in the laboratory, always drawn to the leather books, glass beakers and scientific notes Thomas had strewn about his office. Although she was occasionally allowed to watch Thomas work, her primary task was tending to the werewolves of the laboratory. It tested her limits.

Despite the risk, Thomas insisted on keeping the laboratory door open so Mercy could easily enter to carry out her work. Mercy thought it was far too dangerous, but Thomas assured her only trusted people were permitted inside of the tower. That was a straight lie. Mitchell had been trusted and he had tried to kill her. When she added she didn't want to have to wrangle werewolves again, he replied with a grin that the werewolves were rarely released from their cages without proper precautions. This was another lie.

Thomas released werewolves regularly in his lab, for socializing, for checkups, or to let them stretch their legs. Mercy would remind him when the laboratory door was open and he would act shocked, or ask her to fetch Leyda to close it. She wasn't sure if he was mocking her, or if he was too occupied with his work to notice. In Mercy's shrewd opinion, it was amazing all of Kanta didn't know what he did down in his laboratory.

Each day Mercy grew more comfortable with the werewolves down in the laboratory and she seemed to grow on them too. She assumed it was mostly because she brought them food and changed their bedding, but sometimes they would just sit beside her or lie down at her feet when they were free to roam and she was resting. Some even slept as she attempted to clean around them.

It was late one chilly morning when Mercy stepped through the laboratory entrance and pulled the great metal door to behind her. She walked down the steep incline as the scent of the steam diminished, replaced by the smell of the fresh hay she had put into the cages the day before. The sound of the grinders became muffled, a benefit to her new job she had grown to love. Instead she heard the tapping of claws on metal, the tapping of a great tail against the bars, and even snoring from along the far wall.

Thomas walked toward her as she came around the corner with a smile on his lips. It was odd because normally he allowed the werewolves to wander while he was down here working, talking to them even though they couldn't talk back. What was he up to?

"Ah, Mercy! Excellent timing as usual. These new arms are being a nuisance today." The panel on his new left arm was open and Thomas fiddled with the gears inside, causing his fingers on his left hand to twitch violently. His lazy eye drifted to the side as he grunted in frustration and Mercy followed its direction.

A new cage was in the corner of the room near Thomas's office. The werewolf inside crouched in the back corner looking ready to pounce any instant. She hunkered in the shadows, golden eyes watching them hesitantly.

"We have a new member to our little family. Would you mind getting her some fresh bedding? Maybe some food as well?" He put a screwdriver between his teeth as he fiddled with his arm again.

"Sure," Mercy muttered, staring at the werewolf. The longer she looked at her, the more she tugged on her memory. Something was familiar about the color patterns of her fur, the angle of her ears, and her demeanor. "I might know this one."

He pulled the screwdriver out of his teeth. "Oh?"

She nodded and moved closer. The werewolf gave a warning growl as she approached. Mercy felt the hairs rise on the back of her neck.

"Not well, I assume." He scoffed. "It took some time before I felt she was ready to join the others. I didn't want her to encourage violence, but as you can see, she is still very anxious.

"Who brought her in?"

"Goodness, let's see. I've had her isolated for… a week? No, two weeks."

Mercy felt heat rise to her cheeks. Two weeks ago. Thomas didn't bring in many female werewolves. Most were killed after getting caught by trappers. She looked down and saw the long claws. Her eyes went wide as she remembered the pain across her back. This was the werewolf she and Dad had brought in the day he died.

She heard her pulse pound in her ears and leaned a hand out to press against the cool, solid stone wall. Taking a deep breath, she steadied herself.

"My goodness," Thomas drawled, "whatever is the matter?" Though his words should have reflected concern, no compassion resonated in his voice, only a thin interest.

Thomas could be sympathetic. She had seen that after Dad had died. It always faded the more time he spent on his work. It was as though it sucked away his humanity, until he saw all of them as walking flesh bags.

She took another breath to keep from snapping at him. "She's the one Dad and I brought in together."

"Oh," Thomas whispered. Finally he put away his screwdriver and stepped beside her. "You mean Solomon." No distraction any longer, his voice held only a sadness that resonated with her own. She had forgotten that even though Solomon had been her father, he and Thomas had been friends. Based on what little social life her father had, she had to guess Thomas had been his only friend.

Mercy nodded, unable to find words.

Thomas looked at the werewolf with a shadowed expression. "I am sorry. He deserved better."

"I know he did." She swallowed down the cry that threatened to release into the stone chamber. It should be tears that wanted to escape, but all she felt was fury. Mercy wanted to scream. Her father hadn't even gotten a burial. He was probably in pieces out in those woods, torn apart by the beasts that lived there. There was no grave, no memorial, only her memory.

Neither Thomas or Leyda had asked if she wanted to return home again, and she hadn't volunteered to go. She couldn't bring herself to go back. One day she knew she had to go back and face the pieces of her old life. She knew that, but she didn't want to. She wanted to move past it, to keep her fury for her father's death white hot instead of letting it grow cold. She wanted vengeance, not grief.

"If you want, I can ask Leyda to do it. I completely understand if you don't want to work with her if it brings up bad memories."

Mercy thought of Leyda's words, about how she didn't think she had the stomach for the work and clenched her teeth. "I can do it. You don't have to bother Leyda with it."

Thomas cocked his head to the side and she could practically hear the gears in his head moving. "I wouldn't begrudge you that small luxury. You have been through a lot, I suppose." He was feigning compassion again, trying to solve her like he tried to solve the werewolves in cages. It was uncomfortable being a specimen under his gaze.

She snapped, "I can do it." Her anger bubbled over unexpectedly and she instantly regretted it. She tried her best not to lose her temper, but Thomas could get under her skin far too easily.

He gave a small smirk and put a hand on her shoulder. It felt warm despite the panel that was still open on his forearm exposing the mechanical parts hidden within.

"You remind me so much of your father sometimes, it's uncanny. He too struggled to contain his anger, as you probably know better than most."

Mercy winced. There he was again, pushing his words under her skin like a needle into her bloodstream.

"Just be careful that your anger doesn't end up betraying you. I want to keep you safe here, Mercy. Please don't jeopardize that just to prove something to me."

She nodded. Despite Thomas's cruel words, there was truth to them. He might be cold and analytical at times, but he could read people. Sometimes it felt like he read her mind.

He pulled his hand away and closed the panel on his arm. "I'm going to dig up some food for myself. The prongs are in the corner if you need them. I don't think you will though. That one is all roar and no bite. I think once she realizes we don't want to harm her, she'll calm down."

Mercy turned to watch him leave, but he turned around just before climbing the slope toward the entrance.

"And Mercy, try not to let his death weigh on you. I

know it's hard, but we are doing good work here. If this all succeeds, no one will have to die because of this disease again."

She was left alone to consider his words. It was hard, sometimes, to feel like this work was good or worthwhile. Mercy felt like she was always cleaning up blood, changing out hay, or bringing raw, bloody meat to the caged werewolves. The goal of it all, the one that had almost gotten her transformed to begin with, was a cure for lycanthropy. She wanted to believe it was possible, but sometimes it was difficult. It didn't help that Thomas was so mercurial or that Leyda was so vicious. Sometimes it seemed they only did this because they enjoyed causing harm.

Mercy grabbed a pair of prongs and wound them up to make sure they worked. The blue electric shock that sparked across the spokes made the werewolf in the cage perk up.

"You know what this does," Mercy said as she put it against the bars of an empty metal cage, allowing the electricity to discharge completely before placing it under her arm.

The werewolf's golden eyes followed her every movement, hesitant and fearful. Mercy really hoped she didn't have to zap her, but she knew how fast a werewolf could move and how easy it was to get grievously injured.

Mercy piled up the hay near the cage to make it easier to transfer inside without risking getting hurt. Then she wound up the prongs and stepped toward the she-wolf's cage. The werewolf clamored backwards, clearly terrified, and Mercy felt sorry for her.

"Just stay back," Mercy warned. "I don't want to have to hurt you, but I will if you try anything."

The first few scoops of hay went inside without a problem, and the werewolf remained frozen in place. Mercy felt confident for the first ten rakes or so. Then the werewolf started pacing. She was still on the opposite side of the cage, so Mercy thought it would be harsh to punish her for it. She only had a few feet to really pace in, but she moved faster and faster, turning around with a whimper that grew into a clear panic.

"Calm down. We're almost done," Mercy said. Sweat trickled down the back of her neck.

Then Mercy dropped the rake. When it clattered to the ground, the werewolf jumped with a yelp and lunged forward.

On instinct, Mercy fell backward as a werewolf arm shot through the bars to reach her. Mercy fell hard on her rear, leaning back from the long, sharp claws. Stunned just long enough, she felt the claws scrape along her jaw. She jerked her head back. The fresh pain pulled her to her senses and she remembered the prongs in her hand. With a cry, Mercy shoved the prongs through the bars and into the werewolf's neck. Giving a high-pitched squeal, she was thrown back against the bars of the cage. Mercy scrambled backward. Hot blood dripped down her neck as she panted, shaking from head to toe.

The werewolf curled up on the opposite side of her cage again, whimpering. Mercy got to her feet and put a hand to her jaw to feel the wounds. They weren't deep, but if she had gotten any closer Mercy's throat would be sliced open.

"I warned you, didn't I?" she said to the huddling werewolf, her voice breaking. "Why did you do that?" The werewolf didn't respond, couldn't respond, but Mercy heard an eerie, familiar laughter fill the chamber.

She turned and readied the prongs, already on high alert. "Who's in here?" she demanded. "You better show yourself!"

"I'm exactly where you put me, brat."

Her blood went cold as she turned to see Carter in one of the cages. He looked pale and sickly. His eyes were glassy and his cheekbones hollow, like he hadn't slept for a long time.

Mercy squinted at him, "What happened? I thought you transformed weeks ago?"

He glared at her. "You forget how werewolves work outside of this madman's laboratory?"

Mercy pursed her lips, hating how Carter's mere presence made her question herself. He had that effect on her and he knew it.

"Every damn night I transform and your sick boss comes down to watch! I think he enjoys seeing a man suffer."

"Or maybe just you." Mercy drew herself up taller. "Maybe he just enjoys seeing a jerk like you in pain."

Carter rolled over and pushed his face against the bars and Mercy backed away from him. He had no arms, but he was still dangerous. "Listen, I know you don't like me much, but you can't approve of this. He's going to give me his Liquid Lead tonight. Do you know what that shit will do to me?"

Mercy gripped her prongs. "It'll turn you into a mindless beast, an animal at all hours of the day, but it will make you more controllable too. Maybe he'll hook you up to the mill. Let you run the grinders day and night until you drop."

Carter slammed a shoulder against the bars and the entire cage rattled. "I am *not* going to let him do that to me! I will *not* be reduced to a wild animal."

Mercy lifted her chin. "I think it'll be an improvement."

He pushed himself up—far faster than Mercy expected—and pressed his chest against the bars. "And here I thought you had a damn heart. You approve of him taking away my mind?"

"It's not like there was much there to begin with. I'm glad you're here. Seeing you get tortured is the only reason I stayed."

He bared his teeth, but his eyes glittered with tears. "So I guess he would approve of what you've become? Your old man, I mean."

Mercy felt her entire body go rigid with his words. Her words came out like she had been punched. "What did you say?"

He shook his head, giving a wild grin. "I'm sure old Solomon would be thrilled to see how crazy Thomas Farrell got his claws into you! Is that what he told you before he died? To run here and hide in his freak show?"

Mercy gaped at him, unable to find words.

"What does he call you, a *laboratory* assistant? Let's

be honest here. You and I both know you're not smart enough for that. Your father was known for killing, not for smarts, brat. And your mom? Ha! Let's just say she was known more for her spirits than her brains, okay? You're the kid of a drunk and a psycho." Carter snickered.

Mercy thought of the books her father had made her stitch back together when they fell apart. She thought of him reading the books beside her, how she could pronounce the words better than he could. She might not have had the chance to learn, but she was learning now. She was here to make a change. She clenched the charged prongs in her hands.

"Be real here, brat. Do you really think that madman has your future in mind? Are you stupid enough to believe he's protecting you? He's turned you into his little lap dog and you're too dense to realize it." He gave a high-pitched laugh that made her break out in a sweat. "Solomon would be pissed to see you babysitting Thomas's pet werewolves."

"Stop talking about my parents." She growled. "You have no right to even mention their names. You didn't even know them."

He gave another mad laugh that made Mercy shake with rage. "I had no idea Solomon kept his little girl so sheltered and hidden away. Your father was a monster and everybody knew it. If Mitchell and I had sold you like we intended—"

"*Stop*," Mercy warned.

"—you would have gotten us a pretty penny. We had a buyer all lined up."

"Stop it!" She rushed forward with a scream, her hands over-priming the prongs. Carter was wide-eyed and for all his talk, he was completely unprepared. She jammed the end against the bars and Carter was flung backward with a cry. He fell in a heap in the back corner of the cage, but Mercy was not done. She was sick of him, sick of his laughter, his cruelty, and his constant abuse. She spun up the prongs again, walked around to the back of the cage, and zapped him in the shoulder. He screamed and she smirked.

"I prefer that to your sick laugh."

Carter blinked at her, trying to catch his breath.

"If my father had survived, he would have hunted you down. So I'm only following his lead."

Carter watched her like a trapped animal. She wondered how long Carter had hunted women instead of werewolves, and how many women and children he and Mitchell had trapped and sold.

"How many people did you capture over the years?" she asked, walking casually from one side of the cage to the other. Carter ducked away every time she drew near, shaky and breathless.

"What? I don't know, we didn't keep count!"

She glared at him. "So you did work with Mitchell regularly."

He glowered at her, "Sure, we worked together. All the time! It's not like it matters now. He's dead anyway."

She wound up a nice electric charge between the spokes of the prongs.

Carter whimpered.

"Who was your buyer?"

"What?" He looked between her and the prongs in confusion.

"Was it someone in Kanta? Of course not, you all couldn't risk that, especially with Mitchell working with Thomas. So…who was it?"

He shook his head, sweat beading on his forehead. "I don't know. Mitchell took care of that. Some guy up north."

"I'll need more than that to stop."

"I don't know!"

She placed the electrified prongs closer to the cage.

"I swear!" He screamed, "I don't know who it was! Mitchell didn't trust me enough to tell me!"

"I don't blame him. You're a pretty slimy person, but I believe you."

"You do?" he asked, relaxing a little.

She smiled, then shoved the prongs inside and zapped his shoulder again. Carter cried out. She was about to wind them up again, but a powerful hand grabbed her shoulder and pulled her back.

Mercy fell hard to the floor and the prongs skittered across the ground. Leyda glared at her.

"What are you doing?" she demanded.

Mercy pointed over to Carter, intent on telling her what a horrible person he was, but Carter cowered in the back corner of his cell, his shoulder still smoking from where she zapped him. The words died on her lips. Her fury melted away to embarrassment. All that came out was a string of half-completed statements.

"He was…he said…they kidnapped girls…"

Leyda crossed her arms and shook her head. "Perhaps we were too hasty to let you work here with us, child. You don't seem to understand the importance of our work."

"No, I—"

She held up a hand and Mercy fell silent. "I don't want to hear any of your excuses right now. We need to speak, but upstairs, not here. This is no place to talk freely." Leyda took hold of her arm and jerked Mercy to her feet. "You're bleeding." No concern sounded in her voice, merely an observation.

"The new werewolf. She clawed me."

"I see that."

Mercy clenched her jaw.

Leyda didn't let go of her arm and dragged her over to a corner where a satchel was laid beside the stash of prongs. She picked up the bag, pulled a jar and some gauze out, and pushed the bag at Mercy without a word. Mercy took a deep breath and reached inside to feel more medical supplies inside.

When Leyda applied the salve, it burned, and Mercy had to resist pulling away. Then Leyda began bandaging up her throat, all without a word.

"I'm sorry, I didn't mean to upset you."

Leyda glared at her. "I'm angry that you're abusing your power down here."

Mercy had no words.

"And stop talking. It makes it harder to wrap."

Mercy went quiet and studied the stone wall instead. Behind her she could hear Carter gasping and whimpering in the corner but she couldn't make herself feel sympathy for him. Carter didn't deserve that and Leyda knew it. So why was she so angry with her?

LEYDA PUSHED the large metal door closed with a slam that echoed up and down the walls of the tower. Leyda had done a good job with the bandages. Almost too good since Mercy found them a little tight, though she doubted that was on accident. Leyda turned around to her, and this time Mercy had prepared herself enough to be able to find the words she needed.

"He's a horrible person and deserves to die," she stated as Leyda sat down on the foot of the stairway and removed her headwrap. Unlike the delicate ways that she normally undid them, this time they were forceful and Mercy took a step back as Leyda faced her directly, clearly brimming with anger.

"You are so naïve you don't see anything beyond you, do you, child?"

Mercy blinked and took a deep breath. "You know he's a horrible person. I know you agree with me on that."

Leyda snarled and shook her head, looking far more wolf-like than Mercy liked. "Yes, of course, I agree with you. He is indeed a terrible person, but do you not understand the gravity of what you do when you torture a man down there?"

"I'm making a point. If Thomas gives him Liquid Lead tonight, he loses his mind. He won't be able to give us any answers and he won't suffer any longer. That isn't fair!"

Leyda looked taken back by her words for a moment and didn't respond.

"If you agree with me, then why did you stop me?"

Leyda balled up her wrappings and dropped a hand to her knee. It was a long moment before she finally looked Mercy in the eye. "I could hear his screams echo up the entire tower, child."

A chill went through her.

"Did you know that? I can guess from your face that you didn't. I can hear almost any loud noise you make down there. It doesn't matter where I am in this damn tower, I'll hear you."

Mercy dropped her gaze, fidgeting. It was hard to stand up against Leyda, especially when she was mad. "I didn't realize he was so loud."

"People scream loudly when they are in pain. You should know that from hearing his transformations."

Mercy dropped her hands to her sides.

"I don't think you're aware of it, but you just terrified every other werewolf down there with you. Including the new one who scratched you. Excellent work at gaining her trust."

That was a hard blow, but Mercy didn't want to hear it. She knew she had to be in the right. "Terrified? They're werewolves. They could kill me in an instant if they wanted to. I'm sure they've seen far worse."

"Yes, you are right. I'm sure they have." She sat back against the step with a stern expression. "But they are in cages and you are not."

She shook her head. "No, that's not fair. I didn't mean for that."

"There are children down there, and we aren't sure how old they are. They could be ten, or even five, for all we know."

Her stomach went tight at her words and she had to close her eyes. Leyda reached over and put a hand on her shoulder. Mercy shook her head, not wanting to believe Leyda's words, not wanting to be the person who tortured someone in front of children, but she knew Leyda's words carried truth.

"I know it's easy to think they are monsters who have seen many horrors, but you are their caretaker. As terrible as Carter is, and as much as you want to see him dead, they are as vulnerable as he is. When you harm him, they know you could harm them too."

She opened her mouth to protest.

"Even if you never intend to hurt them. You need to remember that."

Mercy dropped her hands, angry with herself. Leyda was right. She hadn't thought of anyone except herself. If Leyda hadn't shown up, she wasn't sure when she would have stopped. Would it have been before or after Carter stopped screaming? Had the other werewolves been upset by her actions? If they were, she hadn't noticed. She hadn't even cared to look at them.

"I was trying to learn who they sold the women to, and the children. What about all those girls they captured?"

Leyda took a deep breath. "I hate to say this, Mercy, but I believe you appreciate honesty. How many girls your age have you known growing up? And how many young women?"

Mercy shook her head. "You were the first woman I had ever seen, other than a few older women in town. But they all keep to themselves. My father told me that the werewolves favored them, but Thomas told the trappers had actually stolen them away."

Leyda frowned. "Mercy, the only young women in Kanta who are not werewolves are here, and I'm only partially human. Why do you think Thomas is so determined to find a cure? You are foolish if you think you can help those women now. Many were taken when you were just a baby. They have probably been taken far from these lands by now."

"But, Leyda, we have to try! What's the point in me escaping all of that if I can't help anyone? Thomas's work is important, I agree, but all I'm doing is cleaning the mill, feeding werewolves, and changing bedding. I want to do something to really help, not just be cleaning up after him."

Leyda was quiet for a moment before speaking in a soft voice. "Carter got under your skin down there, didn't he?"

Mercy felt the pity in her voice and nodded, trying to ignore the pain in her heart.

"I've told Thomas he's wasting you on such menial tasks." Leyda gave a nod, "Tomorrow I need to go into the woods and I want you to come with me."

"Why?"

She shook her head. "You'll see when we get there." Leyda got to her feet and picked up her wrappings. "You take care of your chores for the rest of the day, and I'll make sure you're free to accompany me." She turned to leave but stopped at the door and looked back.

"And remember, Carter is a small man in a very big world. He means nothing and you shouldn't waste your time or energy on him. Don't go down to speak with him again even if you're tempted to. He may not have his mind for much longer, but you will. He will get under your skin, make you doubt yourself, and get his own petty revenge on you. Don't let him win."

Mercy blinked. She had never considered Carter was saying those things to get back at her, but of course he would. His body was broken, and soon his mind would be too. Attacking Mercy was the only power he had left, if she gave it to him.

"I won't." She felt stronger saying it aloud. "I won't go near him. You're right. He's just desperate, and he won't be around much longer anyway."

Leyda gave her a devious smile. "Good. I hope you are a fast learner."

***

THAT NIGHT MERCY went to her room, knowing that Thomas intended to give Carter the Liquid Lead. What he planned to do with him after, she didn't know and she didn't want to know. Part of her wanted to go down into the laboratory and watch him lose his mind completely, knowing Thomas would fully permit it. But the other part of her didn't.

Leyda was right. She didn't need to waste her time

on Carter anymore. He was trying to get to her, to get under her skin and hurt her even more than he already had. He wouldn't have his mind long, so he would force Mercy to suffer instead. By going down there, Carter would know he won in the end, and she couldn't let him do that. By staying away from him, she was proving he was worth nothing. That would be her victory.

Instead, she bedded down, listening to the grinders working, and breathed in the steam of the mill. For the first time since her arrival, she dreamed peaceful dreams. She didn't let Carter disrupt her thoughts more than he already had that day. Instead she thought of her father reading aloud to her by candlelight in the wee hours of the evening. She remembered his laugh and his rare, warm smile.

Perhaps her father was truly avenged. Perhaps now she could move forward and build a new life for herself.

She could almost hear Carter's screams deep in the laboratory as his humanity dwindled away. In her dreams she ran through the forest of her childhood with sunlight filtering down through the trees.

3

THE WOLF OF KANTA

MERCY WOKE the next morning to sunlight gleaming in through the windows. The wind couldn't be very strong today because the steam wasn't rising like normal, but hung low in the air. It made the air humid and thicker than normal. The sheets felt too heavy on her skin. The grinder noise was never-ending. It drove her mad the first few nights, but now she found it oddly comforting. She slept to the rhythmic sound, she worked with it almost always filling the background, and she was now accustomed to the unique smell of oil and dirt. It was in complete contrast to the life she had once known, and somehow that felt good.

Gone were the days of doing household chores and preparing for her father's return. She didn't need to wake at dawn to make her father breakfast or tend to his supplies or repairs. No one woke her in the morning, or timed her speed, or stood over her throughout the day. Neither Thomas nor Leyda monitored her tasks as long as she finished her work. They simply relied on her to do her job and do it well.

Sometimes she still woke in the middle of the night, waking from panicked nightmares of the barrier being down or her father home from a hunt and demanding to be cared for. She felt such relief when she realized she didn't live there anymore, it made her feel guilty.

Yet as much as she felt guilt for her own relief and tried to convince herself otherwise, her life had improved since she arrived at the mill. She no longer had to endure Dad's drunken rages and unexpected beatings. Life with him had been hard, painful, unpredictable, and full of tears. For the first time in her life, Mercy could discover what she enjoyed doing instead of what she needed to do. She could prove she was valuable outside of merely supporting someone else.

She proved herself to Leyda once already and earned the right to join her in a trip into the woods today. Mercy was nervous. She hadn't been into those woods since her father died, since she was chased by Carter and Mitchell, but she was eager to prove herself and try something new. Something more than cleaning cages and repairing walls. Something that would make people like Carter think twice before calling her a brat.

Mercy fetched some water from the bedside carafe. Though lukewarm, it felt good on her throat. She stared out at the billows of steam settling against the ground and the cloudy sky above.

Leyda saw promise in her, and Mercy wanted to prove she was right. Yet only a couple of weeks ago

Leyda would have happily had Mercy down in that cage in Carter's place. It would have been her bones breaking instead of his.

She sipped at her water and thought about him getting the Liquid Lead. She wouldn't have been much better off than the werewolves in the cages if she had taken his place. She needed to prove her worth. She needed to show she was more than a test subject.

She put her glass down on the table.

Her father would never let her do much. It was always cooking, cleaning, preparing his tools, and occasionally lessons, but those had taken a backseat to his profession. It had to really, if they were to survive, but Mercy bristled under his control. She remembered a day much like this one, when she asked if she could go with him to help hunt werewolves, but he sneered and shook his head. She persisted every morning when he got home from work. Eventually he had agreed. Maybe it was because she was beginning to look like a woman, maybe she reminded him of her mother, or maybe she had annoyed him enough. It didn't matter, she would never know the real reason. That thought stung, but she shook it away.

He always had some excuse. Even if they hadn't been attacked on the way back, he was already deciding she was a hindrance. She was too slow to get back to the truck or too young to draw in a male werewolf in the dead of night. Would she have ever earned his respect? Would he have ever embraced her as an apprentice instead of a child?

She would never know the answer and that pain weighed heavily on her shoulders. She got to her feet and sponged off with the bowl of bathing water. She pulled on her blouse and linen pants and put up her hair.

She needed to focus on the day ahead. Dwelling in the past slowed her down and gave people like Carter power. That bastard had taken enough from her already.

———

AS MERCY DESCENDED the spiral staircase, she spotted Thomas standing in front of the kitchen door, a piece of bread in one hand and one of his notebooks in the other. He had buttoned up his white shirt crooked, making his collar too high on one side. His red hair was pulled back without his usual care and he had dark circles under his eyes that were pronounced on his pale skin. He also wasn't wearing his signature red cape. That was unusual, even for him.

He didn't look up as Mercy came to his landing.

"How did it go with Carter last night, Mr. Farrell?"

One eye shot up to her while the lazy eye pointed stubbornly down at the notebook. "Ah yes, Mercy. Good morning." He gave a wane smile. "It went well enough, I suppose, but not as planned. I was hoping my new experimental formula would allow Carter to retain his mind, but against all my expectations, it didn't."

"So he's lost then," Mercy said, a jolt of joy coursing

through her knowing Carter's mind was lost. Then she instantly felt bad for feeling it.

"I'm afraid so." He shook his head. "I'm afraid it only caused him more pain, which was the opposite of what I wanted. Now I'm not certain if that was due to his extreme injuries, a bad formula, or some other factor I haven't considered." He took a bite of his pastry.

She glanced to the notebook in his hand, at the folded corners, the pages sticking out of it. As much as Mercy was glad to hear that Carter had suffered, she knew it wasn't good news. If the research hadn't worked for Carter, then that meant there was no cure, and Thomas was once again without a test subject. "So what does that mean for your research?"

Thomas gave a heavy sigh and shrugged, blinking his bloodshot eyes. "It means I need to find someone else to be a test subject."

She took an involuntary step back.

"No, not you, Mercy! You've been a big help for us. It was probably cruel to force someone to become a werewolf, but I was certain that we had a cure this time." He glanced down the steps as though gleaning where she was going. "Wait, Leyda is heading into the woods today, isn't she?"

Mercy nodded.

"And you're going with her, correct?"

"Yes, but I don't understand—"

"Excellent!" He went forward and put a hand on her shoulder. "I think you'll be an excellent partner for her today. Leyda doesn't get out very much, as you can imagine, so I'm glad to see you two are bonding."

Mercy gave a nervous laugh. "I don't know if bonding is the right word," she admitted. "But she is tolerating me."

"That's more than she does for me, Mercy." He laughed.

She shook her head. "But I don't understand. What does this have to do with your experiment?"

"Leyda will explain everything to you, don't worry." He glanced down to the base of the stairs again before lowering his voice. "To be honest, I worry that I'm losing my skill at this. Please don't let on to Leyda. She is hellbent on me finding a cure. But this is lycanthropy we're talking about. It's a disease that has been around for millennia without a cure. The possibility of making great change is very low, especially considering my lack of training. The limitations of Kanta, you understand."

Mercy glanced down the steps and spotted Leyda in the distance sorting through something in the corner. "You made Liquid Lead. It's the only thing known to affect them other than silver bullets. Don't doubt yourself. You're a genius."

"Genius a strong word," he said, pursing his lips. "I believe I have more of a mind for gears and steam than I do for chemical compounds."

"I think you're being too hard on yourself. Maybe you didn't give Carter enough or gave him too little. You can't beat yourself up over one failure."

He grinned. "My goodness, I do appreciate your enthusiasm. Perhaps in a few months after you've gained your feet more, you'll be on the front lines helping directly with my experiments. Would you like that?"

Mercy tried not to notice Thomas also thought she wasn't fully ready for the work at the mill. She focused on the opportunity instead of the judgment. She so wanted to prove him and Leyda wrong. "I would like to try," she said.

Saying the words aloud felt like it made it more possible. Excitement filled her because the thought of working alongside Thomas in the laboratory with his chemicals, beakers, and books was so different from anything she had been trusted with before. She imagined standing beside him, materials in hand, finally respected and appreciated for all the work she did. Maybe working at the mill could give her the confidence and respect she had so dearly craved her entire life, something she could never hope to get from her father.

MERCY WENT DOWN the spiral staircase to the ground floor where Leyda was working. The pile of things she had seen her rummaging through from above was actually a pile of clothes. She stifled a laugh.

"Is it laundry day?" she asked, still a little giddy from getting the opportunity to study with Thomas.

Leyda glared at her. "No, it isn't laundry day. Thomas hires workers for that, as you know."

Mercy's smile faded as she folded her arms and leaned against the stairwell. She had hoped Leyda would be in better spirits, but she seemed angrier than normal. "You're right, I'm sorry."

Leyda gestured to Mercy's work pants and blouse,

the uniform she wore everyday since she started working at the mill. "That, what you're wearing, that won't work. You'll need to change."

"What's wrong with this?"

"You look too much like a woman and we can't have that. You'll be noticed by every person we pass. No, if we want to get through the city and into the woods during the day, we need to both pass as men."

Mercy looked down at the pile of clothing with concern. She wasn't sure how all the clothing in the world was going to help with that. "With these? You really think these will help?" She picked up a pair of faded leather pants that looked like they had been worn out by three people before landing here.

"I'll show you, child. If you want to travel through the city of Kanta during the day, you'll need a proper disguise. One that even your father wouldn't recognize."

Mercy winced. Her father would have been absolutely outraged at her pretending to be a man. Even though in retrospect that might have saved her a lot of trouble in Kanta, and possibly even saved his life.

Leyda shifted through the clothes, through bundled up linen shirts and strips of torn fabric. She picked up a pair of men's black pants and nodded. "Take off your clothes and leave them on the stairs."

"Wait. Here?" She glanced around but Thomas was no longer on the landing above, though she noticed the door to the laboratory was still open.

"Yes, here. Thomas went down to the lab and there's no one else in the tower today. Do you think I would ask you to do such a thing in full display?"

"No," Mercy said and quickly changed into the new pair of pants. They were far too long, but Leyda wordlessly reached down and rolled up the pant legs. They looked ridiculous.

"Are you sure this is going to work?"

"It will take more than a pair of pants to complete the disguise, but I think it will work, yes."

Leyda let her keep her blouse and worked around it instead. She wrapped long strips of fabric around her, binding down her chest. It wasn't very comfortable, but Mercy had to admit it did make her look more like a man.

"I hope I can breathe in this," she muttered with worry.

"If you complain less, you shouldn't have a problem." Leyda glared. "Now take a deep breath."

Mercy did as she was told and Leyda made a final tight wrapping. When Mercy exhaled, the bandages were much looser and more comfortable, but still held firm. Leyda put a brown tunic over her head to cover everything, and fastened a belt at her waist.

"There we go." She took a step back. Most of Mercy's body was covered beneath thick wraps of fabric and linen. She felt like she was bundled up for winter under so many layers, but Leyda still wasn't pleased. She shook her head and took in a breath.

"What's wrong now?" Mercy asked.

"You have very striking eyes."

Mercy blinked. "Thank you?"

"No, that makes it more difficult to blend in. People

will recognize those eyes. All the spare clothing in the world can't hide them."

Taken aback, Mercy watched as Leyda bent down to look through the clothing some more. She had never thought much about her appearance until the day her father brought her into town with the werewolf in tow. She had never cared much about her appearance. She only cared about what she could do. She was good at dipping needles in Liquid Lead, at keeping the cage and weapons cleaned, and at growing fruits and vegetables in the household garden. She had wanted to be a good werewolf hunter once upon a time, but that chance had already passed her by. Even the guests her father had brought to the house said she was a fine child, but never commented about her looks.

Only when she heard Carter's comments in downtown Kanta had she been keenly aware of her appearance. Her father had warned her of the kind of men who lived in Kanta, but all the warnings in the world couldn't have prepared her for Carter's question asking if she was for sale. She had never felt so uncomfortable in her skin, or so vulnerable just for existing.

As Leyda wrapped dusty fabric around her mouth, nose, and forehead, Mercy was oddly grateful. She remembered how she felt the last time she walked freely in Kanta—and what it ultimately led to. She wanted to be someone else, someone that people would avoid. That was safer.

Finally Leyda wrapped a cloak around her shoulders and pulled the hood down low, just above her eyes.

"I can hide everything except your eyes, child, so it will be up to you to make yourself forgettable."

"Forgettable?" Mercy asked, the dusty fabric around her mouth scratched at her lips, muffling her words.

Leyda nodded. "I don't recommend speaking, unless you're confident you can sound like a man."

Mercy tried to lower her voice some and Leyda winced.

"Maybe you should just stay quiet. Pretend that you're mute or that talking to anyone is beneath you."

"But who are we supposed to be? You're not telling me anything."

She put a hand to her head, giving a frustrated sigh. "If you would listen more and ask fewer questions, I'll tell you."

Mercy clutched her hands together. "Sorry, I'm nervous. The last time I walked through town, my father was killed and I almost died."

Leyda's gaze softened. "You have every right to be nervous. I suppose I'm not used to teaching anyone. I've done this on my own for so long I forget how terrifying it can be at the start. I forget what it was like to feel that vulnerable, that afraid, but I do understand."

Mercy narrowed her eyes. "Surely you're nervous about being found out by them, I mean, looking like you do."

Her eyes crinkled with a smile. "To be honest, a part of me hopes they do find me out one day. I'd rip them apart before they could even pull their guns free from their holsters. And even if they did shoot me, the odds of them carrying silver rounds?" She laughed and

Mercy felt a chill go down her spine. "But you're right, getting shot isn't fun. The less we make ourselves, or Thomas, a target, the better."

"Why Thomas?"

"Because he gives us a safe space to live. If the trappers in Kanta knew what he did or who he had down here, this entire building would go up in flames. Getting shot would be a mercy compared to what he would face."

Mercy's eyes went wide.

"You'll be with me, child, remember that. You'll have no need to fear with me nearby."

Mercy swallowed down the dry patch in her throat. Leyda was confident in her abilities, but the last time she was shot, she was incapacitated, unable to help Mercy or Thomas. Leyda had her strength and her ferocity, but Mercy had no such protection. If she had learned anything from her father, it was to never rely on others to keep her safe.

Kneeling down, she sorted through the pile until she found what she was looking for: a belt with a holster. She undid the belt Leyda had put around her waist and dropped it to the floor, replacing it with the new one.

Leyda stiffened.

"Look, I know it makes you uncomfortable, but I'm not going out there without protection. I don't have your strength to tear off limbs or Thomas's metal arms to take a bullet. If I get found out, I'm captured and sold, it's as simple as that. I've nearly been eaten by a pack of werewolves once, and never want to experience that again. So even if you don't like it, I will need silver bullets."

She looped the belt up and glanced up to meet Leyda's eyes. She was expecting to see frustration tinged with fear in those eyes, but instead she found something very different: respect.

"I think I know where I can find a pistol for you, and the *silver* bullets you request." She sneered. Even saying the words clearly upset her. She leaned forward, bringing her face mere inches from Mercy's, and Mercy leaned away from her. "I will give you one warning and that is all I will ever give. If you ever raise a gun at me, I will rip your throat out faster than you can scream for help. Do you understand?"

Mercy stared into her caramel eyes and shook from head to toe with fear. It was like facing that werewolf in the woods again, but so much worse because she knew Leyda meant it. She had seen her kill. She had cleaned up the body left behind. Mitchell hadn't lasted long once Leyda decided to kill him. Leyda was truly bloodthirsty, and it was wiser to be her friend than her enemy.

Mercy gave a quick nod as she sweated through the fabric on her forehead. Leyda pulled back, her eyes crinkling with a vicious smile.

"Good. Now we have that settled, I'll fetch those for you so we can head out. This will take some time and I don't want us to lose daylight."

When Leyda was gone, Mercy put a hand out to the stairway railing to steady herself. Just when she felt like she was making progress, Leyda put her back in her place. If this was what bonding felt like, Mercy didn't like it.

———

IT WAS STRANGE to walk out of the mill and into the dusty streets of Kanta again. The last time she had been here, Mercy was naïve and inexperienced. She was a girl trying to prove she could be a werewolf hunter, oblivious to the dangers that surrounded her. She had tried to show off to her father and instead she had made herself a target for hunters. How her entire world had changed in a matter of weeks!

The layers of clothing she wore were already hot despite the chilly breeze that had finally picked up. Above, the clouds had parted to reveal a crisp, blue autumn sky, and the humidity that had felt so close when she awoke had finally dissipated.

Mercy felt like a different person and Leyda's disguise only added to it. The outfit felt like armor. She received no curious looks through cracks in shutter windows, or any lewd commentary from passers-by. She was a hunter, one of the many nameless faces that wandered through Kanta every day looking for easy money. At first she wasn't sure if it would work, but as they walked down Main Street, she wondered why her father never considered disguising her. Then again, he would scoff at his daughter dressing as a boy. She shook her head as his voice came to mind.

No daughter of mine is going to humiliate me by pretending to be a boy!

His imagined outrage only fueled her determination.

The pistol on her hip also helped, hidden between folds of fabric for easy reach. She didn't dare confess to Leyda she was a bad shot, but coming out onto the streets again with a real weapon, instead of some pathetic prongs, gave her far more confidence. Would she actually be able to draw the weapon if she needed it? She hoped she wouldn't have to find out. The memory of the gunshot that killed her father still haunted her nightmares. She would never forget the sound or the echo.

Mercy hadn't paid much attention to her surroundings last time. She had been too focused on impressing her father, on doing her job right, and proving that she could be a werewolf hunter. This time she noticed the buildings they passed. The pub looked like it was just opening up as bar stools were removed from tables. They moved past a busy looking inn that she hadn't even known existed in Kanta. Of course, that was probably where most of the hunters came in to see if they could make a living trapping werewolves. The idea of anyone wanting to visit Kanta was bewildering.

When the jailhouse came into view Mercy felt her heart beat faster. A short man with pallid skin, a sunburned face, and a white beard eyed them as he leaned against the wooden wall. The building had no windows and the front door was propped open, revealing a shadowy room within.

"Remember, let me do the talking," Leyda said in a deep voice that sounded nothing like her normal one.

"Will do," Mercy answered, deciding to go for a hoarse whisper to hide her high-pitched voice.

Leyda gave the briefest of nods and Mercy couldn't help but smile to herself. She had wondered if she was put on the spot if she could come up with some voice decent enough to get Leyda's approval. She was picky, but maybe someone else wouldn't be.

As they approached the jailhouse, the man pushed himself off of the wall and moved toward the street, clearly intending to intercept them. One hand swung at his side, but his other gripped his belt, not far from the gun he openly wore on his hip. Mercy pursed her lips together.

"Not often I see a pair of new faces around here." The man glared at the two of them. His eyes moved between them quickly, as though looking for a reason to draw his weapon.

Leyda spoke in her deep voice. "You must be mistaken, Mr. Pillsby. I thought I introduced myself a few weeks back." She extended a gloved hand. "The name is Luke, sir. Mr. Farrell hired me to help him out with a few things around the mill." She gestured to Mercy. "And this is my business associate, Mark."

Mercy nodded her head but didn't extend a hand. She was afraid it would give her away.

The man gave a thin smile. "It's Jacob, not Mr. Pillsby. If we met before, then you ought to know that."

If Leyda was thrown off by his comment, she didn't show it. Instead she shrugged. "My apologies, I tend to be formal around law enforcement, sir."

Jacob nodded and put a hand to his beard, looking

them both up and down. "A pair of hunters? An odd choice to get a position with Thomas."

Leyda scoffed. "I don't pretend to understand him. Thomas is an odd man."

That made Jacob give a genuine smile. "You're not wrong there. Regardless of whether we've met before, you and your friend will need to fill out some forms before I can let you do any trapping in the forest around Kanta. I'm not sure where you two are from, but you should know the woods are dangerous here. We have a strict curfew after dark, and we keep a list of names of hunters in town. You know, just in case something happens."

Mercy had to clench her teeth to keep from saying anything. Law enforcement was quick to take down names of hunters when they faced werewolves, but where was their concern when all the young women and girls were captured and sold into servitude? She doubted they had paperwork on any of the women who had been taken in Kanta. Where was the concern about her father's death? She guessed it was easier to fill out forms than it was to investigate the real horrors going on in the city.

As Jacob turned to lead them inside, Mercy glanced to Leyda. Despite her calm facade, fear perched in her eyes. What would happen if they were found out? It was one thing getting attacked out in the open, but in close quarters, things could turn dangerous quickly. Despite Leyda's confidence, they had both seen how eager Jacob was to pull his gun. Even if they didn't use silver bullets, Mercy had seen how a single gunshot affected her. She wasn't sure what would happen to her if Leyda was brought down, but she imagined it involved a jail cell and possibly being sold if Jacob needed the extra money. Someone who was friends with a partially transformed werewolf would not be seen as friendly.

Stepping through the doorway of the jailhouse, Mercy felt her stomach clench. A putrid mixture of body odor, stale beer, and the distant scent of urine permeated the air. A few desks sat out on either side of the door, but all the seats were empty. Beyond the desks was a long, narrow hallway and cells lined both walls. She could see many figures through the bars. The jail looked almost full. Somebody in the distance sounded like they were hacking up a lung. Leyda had stepped inside confidently enough, but bent down to put a shaky hand on the desk. Her eyes were closed and Mercy could hear her breathing hard. Was she going to collapse? Thinking quickly, Mercy pulled over a chair from one of the other desks so Leyda could sit. The wooden legs squealed across the floor and echoed throughout the jailhouse.

Jacob didn't seem to notice. He was riffling through papers across the room, going through a huge stack that leaned against the wall. While the prisoner in the back started hacking again, Mercy leaned down to Leyda's ear and whispered, "Are you okay?"

Leyda nodded with her eyes still closed. Sweat soaked the bandages on her brow and across her nose. She looked like she might be physically ill if she stayed. Was it the smell or something else?

"Let me handle this," Mercy whispered.

Leyda looked at her with concern. "Are you sure?"

To be honest, she wasn't, but if Leyda lost herself here, they could both be in major trouble. Their disguises would be lost, and Jacob could easily overpower Mercy. So despite her own racing heartbeat, Mercy nodded.

Leyda didn't argue or resist. She knew the consequences would be worse for her. She got up and left quickly with barely a sound.

"Ah, here we go!" Jacob called from across the room. "Took me forever to find the blasted—" He turned and realized Leyda was gone. His right hand dropped to the holster on his hip and drew the weapon out in a single, fluid motion, aiming it at Mercy.

Mercy's stomach dropped, but she tried to mimic her father's nonchalance. "There's no need for all that, Luke had to step outside is all," Mercy hissed out in a hoarse whisper.

Jacob looked from her, to the doorway, to the cells, then back again. His gun shook in his hand and his eyes were wide.

She rolled her eyes in exaggeration even as sweat dripped down her back and into the bindings around her chest. "He thought he was going to puke from how gross this place smells. The man has a weak stomach."

"Oh!" Jacob finally relaxed his weapon and gave a chuckle. Mercy could still feel her pulse thrumming in her temples. He holstered his gun again. "Boy, I'm glad you said something, I was thinking it was a jailbreak and was about to blow you away!" He gave a hearty laugh and dropped down in his chair.

Mercy gave a short nod, going against her instinct to scream at him. She was sweating so much she felt one of the wrappings plaster against her forehead. She tried not to think about how close she had come to getting shot again, or about her anger at once again having a gun aimed at her, or about how it made her think of her father. She sat down in the chair she had brought over for Leyda, glad to get off her shaky legs.

Jacob was talking about something, rules that werewolf hunters were supposed to follow, procedures for capturing werewolves, locations permitted for caged werewolves, but Mercy wasn't listening. She knew them all by heart anyway. Her father had drilled them into her head years ago.

Two pages slid toward her across the table and Mercy looked down at them in a haze. She saw their fake names listed on each one. Apparently they didn't care about surnames, which only seemed suspicious. But it was Kanta, so what else was new? At the top in formal handwritten print read: City of Kanta Werewolf Hunter License. Her eyes went wide.

Sure, her name wasn't right and she wasn't even interested in hunting werewolves anymore, but the words made her shiver. She was about to be an official werewolf hunter. Years ago, even weeks ago, that was the only thing she had wanted. Before the world had collapsed around her. Just seeing the form filled her with a familiar excitement. It was a foolish, childish feeling, she knew that, but she couldn't repress that flutter of joy as she picked up the pen to sign.

Then she paused.

No, she couldn't sign it as Mercy Pinkerton. As far as Jacob knew, that girl died in the woods months ago. And in truth, she did die.

Mercy wasn't the same person anymore. It was bittersweet to realize that she had lost that naïve, vulnerable girl she had been, but she had no intention of ever going back to it.

She turned to Leyda's form and wrote Luke in her best printed handwriting. On her own form, she wrote the first thing she thought of: The Wolf of Kanta.

Jacob turned his head to the side, giving a ridiculous laugh as he read it. "Wolf of Kanta, huh? Aren't you a cocky fellow, Mark?"

Mercy got to her feet. "I'm a hunter, Jacob. To hunt a wolf you have to think like a wolf."

Jacob's laughter faded.

"I track and hunt my prey. To hunt them down, I must understand them. It's not too different from you hunting criminals, I'm sure." She leveled Jacob with a cold glare her father would be proud of. Jacob cleared his throat and looked away. "I hunt down the real wolves."

Jacob's voice cracked. "I guess you don't have any questions then?"

"One last one, Jacob. Are we done here or can Luke and I get some real work done?"

Luke put a hand up and gave a nervous laugh. "No, we're all good here, son. You two are free to go about your way."

Mercy nodded and got to her feet. "Oh, and Jacob? I am not a boy or your son. Don't address me as such."

Jacob's face reddened. "Of course, sorry about that, Mark. No disrespect intended!"

Mercy nodded and stepped outside. She breathed in the clean air, feeling more in control of her life than she had in a long time.

The Wolf of Kanta hunting down the real wolves. She liked the sound of that.

4

THE REAL MONSTER

NEITHER MERCY OR LEYDA said a word as they walked deeper into the woods and away from town. Mercy let Leyda lead, but she couldn't help the nervousness she felt at walking through the forest. The last time she was here she was nearly food for the werewolves, and before that she had been chased by Carter and nearly killed. Now it was daytime, with birds chirping, and beautiful beams of sunlight filtered through the branches of the trees. The summer crickets were gone, and the forest floor was littered with piles of leaves. A wind raked through the forest, not quite cold yet, but still, Mercy shivered.

The world had moved on. That was the painful truth of it. The world didn't stop turning, the seasons continued to plow forward, and the trauma of that day had been swept beneath the leaves. Mercy took a deep breath of the breeze, let it fill her lungs, and then let it out. She had to move on too. She couldn't live forever in the past. Dad was dead. Nothing would change that.

Mitchell too, and Carter would likely never have his mind again. The woods of Kanta were safe despite her urge to run back to town.

Only once Kanta was no longer visible behind them and the forest had swallowed them whole did Leyda finally speak. "You handled that officer well," she said. "I expected you to need more help. I thought you might bring him outside to talk."

Mercy wasn't sure why she bristled under Leyda's words. Perhaps it was being back in the woods, or perhaps it was the knowledge that she was still being underestimated. "I'm not as sheltered as everyone assumes I am. I can handle my own when I'm given the chance."

"Hmm." Leyda glanced back, her eyes crinkling in a smile. "How old are you again?"

"Thirteen," Mercy answered.

Leyda scoffed and shook her head. "Old enough to know better but not old enough to listen."

Mercy glared at her. "There's no need to be rude. You were thirteen before too, weren't you?"

Leyda went silent. Not that it was a surprise. Anytime Mercy tried to bring up something about her background, Leyda clamped quiet. If it wasn't talking about tearing off Thomas's arms, then she didn't like to talk about it.

"You know," Mercy said, feeling aggravation creep into her voice. "If you had told me we would be signing up to be licensed werewolf hunters, I would have jumped at the opportunity. I always wanted to be a werewolf hunter when I was little. My father was grooming me to join his work."

Leyda stopped and leaned against a tree, shaking her robe to cool off her body. "Such arrogance. You would be hunting my kind. People who don't deserve to be hunted and killed. Surely you're not so naïve to still be excited by such a cruel concept?"

Mercy pursed her lips. When she thought of werewolves, she thought of the creature she had faced in the woods, or the vicious beasts tethered to the grinders in the mill. Even though she had encountered many who were relatively docile, it was easy to forget that they were still people and not monsters or animals. They were either dosed with Liquid Lead and relatively docile, or they were out to kill her. It was hard to conceive of anything besides that, but Leyda was right. They were human despite what had become of them. Without intending it, her old prejudices still emerged from years of living under Dad's roof and his rules. She once considered him an expert werewolf hunter. She wondered if she would ever shake the indoctrination of growing up as a hunter.

She looked around at the trees as they moved deeper into the forest. They weren't randomly walking, they were following a vague path, one that looked like it had been taken before. The further they walked, the more clear the path became.

"Where are we going?" Mercy asked.

"To see some old friends of mine," Leyda said, pulling her mask down to drink from a waterskin.

"They're werewolves, aren't they?"

Leyda frowned at her as she closed her waterskin. "Why yes, Mercy, they are. How astute of you."

Mercy looked up at the sun almost directly above them. "If I had known that, I would have brought more weapons."

Leyda's eyes went wide as she spun around, far too fast for human reflexes, and aimed a gloved finger at her. "If you dare draw a gun on my friends during the light of day, I will tear your throat out myself!"

Mercy froze. Part of her knew she deserved the threat. She was wrong to say that, to even think it. The other part of her still quaked under Leyda's fury just as she had when they first met.

Leyda wiped at her jaw. "I thought you had potential, but you get excited at signing a werewolf hunting license. You talk of wanting to kill my friends! I should have left you scrubbing the walls at the mill rather than trust you with such a delicate mission."

Mercy threw her hands up. "Look, I'm sorry! I shouldn't have said that, you're right. But you talk down to me all the time! I'm here trying to learn, trying to do better, and always trying to prove myself to you. I was groomed by a werewolf hunter, and what I was taught was wrong. It's going to take me some time to get used to all this."

"Your anger is worse than your father's." Leyda snarled.

Mercy winced. "I'm sorry, but you keep pushing me. You keep me in the dark all the time. I can't just blindly follow you into everything. I need you to talk to me." She pointed back to the path they had taken. "You needed my help back there at the jailhouse. Fortunately I fooled them and there wasn't a problem, but if you don't tell me anything, how am I supposed to help? What if it doesn't go so well next time?"

Leyda snorted and shook her head. "You think too much of yourself. I could have handled the pompous fool without your aid."

"Jacob? Yeah sure, but you would have passed out in that building, and then what?"

Leyda snarled, curling her fingers at her sides. "You aggravate me, child."

"And you terrify me." Mercy's voice rang out amid the trees. Leyda blinked, as though taken aback. Mercy took a moment to catch her breath and keep herself from unloading on Leyda. It was too easy to say the wrong words. Finally she continued, "If I do something good, you rarely thank me. If I do something bad, you threaten to kill me. How do you honestly expect me to learn anything from you?"

Leyda took a step back, avoiding Mercy's gaze. They were both in the wrong, but Mercy felt she had at least apologized. She doubted Leyda would give her anything close to an apology. All she could hope for was a respite from constantly being insulted, berated, or threatened.

"You have to trust me and I have to trust you if this is going to work. It has to come from both sides. Otherwise we might not make it to your friends today."

Leyda didn't respond. Instead she glowered, as if her gaze alone could cause Mercy to spontaneously combust. It was going to take more than words for Leyda to give her another chance.

"You don't trust me still, I understand. If you want, I can leave my gun here." Mercy unsnapped her holster and pulled out the pistol.

Leyda shook her head in absolute confusion.

"Or I can give it to you if you want. If that would help." Mercy held the gun out with both hands and waited for a response. Leyda couldn't be silent on this. She had to choose something. She had to put some trust in Mercy or take it away entirely. She couldn't just resort to anger and threats. She had to prove she was going to try. If she took away the gun, then there was no point in either of them trying to work together any more. Mercy might as well return to the mill and go clean out cages. But if she let her keep the gun, then maybe they did have a chance. It was a big risk.

Leyda watched her for a long moment before reaching out and pushing the offered gun away.

"Keep it, just in case. You are a sheep traveling into a den of wolves. I should keep your fear in mind and maybe cut back on my threats to you. However despite what you say, you are quite sheltered and speak out of turn. You need proper lessons in manners, not the vile teachings of a bloodthirsty werewolf hunter."

Mercy holstered the gun. "Maybe you can teach me that too?"

Leyda barked a laugh. "I don't think so, child. Some battles are not worth fighting."

Mercy nodded, trying not to laugh. "Thank you for giving me another chance. I'll try not to disappoint you again."

Giving a deep sigh Leyda turned back to the path.

"You should care less about disappointing people and more about what is right. Otherwise you'll be doomed to repeat mistakes."

THE PATH that was once clear dwindled the deeper they went into the forest. Moving slowly, they picked their way through thick underbrush and tall weeds. The path wasn't as well maintained or perhaps as well traveled this far away, which seemed strange. Leyda leaped over a decaying log with hardly any effort, but Mercy had to climb over it instead. Leyda had to give her a hand as she got back down to the ground.

"Thank you," Mercy whispered.

Leyda silently nodded before pulling out her waterskin again. "Thomas had another breakthrough after Carter's transformation. Surely you noticed."

"He told me it didn't work as he planned. He said he was back to square one, and that his mixture only made Carter feel more pain during the transformation." Mercy pulled out her own waterskin and pulled down the wrappings around her mouth to drink. She was careful not to talk of Thomas's offer, of the possibility that he would let her assist with his work. Considering their earlier argument, Mercy thought that would be unwise.

Leyda studied her with an intense gaze. "He told you that?"

Mercy gave a short nod, trying not to show her shock at Leyda's response. Had Thomas told her more than Leyda expected? She put away her waterskin and waited for a response.

Finally Leyda gave a short nod. "Regardless of whether it was successful or not, it was a breakthrough. That was one failed direction, but it means another will open up. We are one step closer to a cure, a *real* cure, not this pathetic half-life I have." She balled her fists at her side before closing her eyes, taking a breath, and unfurling her hands. "He only needs one more volunteer in order to find a final solution."

Mercy continued forward, forcing Leyda to walk beside her side. "Do you really think he's that close, or do you think he's leading you on?"

Leyda grabbed her arm and pulled her back. Mercy gave a cry more out of surprise than pain, and suddenly she was staring into Leyda's dark eyes.

"Don't you dare bring that talk to me, child. His work is all that I have left. I won't let you waltz in and take that glimmer of chance away from me. He is close. He told me as much."

Mercy gaped at her, trying to pull her arm away, but Leyda wouldn't let go. "I'm sorry, please. I didn't mean anything by it." Again she had said the wrong words, and again she had angered Leyda.

"No, of course you didn't, *werewolf hunter*." She snarled then released Mercy's arm and took a step back, never withdrawing her gaze.

Rubbing at her arm, Mercy kept her mouth shut. Despite her attempt to force Leyda's trust earlier, it clearly hadn't worked. Everything Mercy said was wrong and instead of building a relationship or even starting a conversation with the woman, she seemed to only make things worse. Perhaps it was better to watch instead of speak for awhile. Otherwise Leyda might desert her in the woods with no way of finding a path back home. Come nightfall, she would be as good as dead.

She thought back her encounter with Thomas that morning. She hadn't missed the exhaustion in his eyes. He hadn't had a breakthrough like Leyda hoped. He had been beaten down. The new test subject would likely not be the last, and yet Leyda clung to every scrap of hope she could, desperate for relief from her cursed existence. Was Thomas actively lying to her, or did Leyda know and just not care? The more Mercy got to know these two, the more confusing they became.

They traveled in silence until the dense trees began to open up. In the distance sunlight beamed through a canopy and once again a clear path was visible. There were odd signs of life of more than just animals. An old jacket littered with holes was barely visible in the tall grass except for a single sleeve that stood up, flapping in the wind. Farther in, a broken whiskey bottle buried in the dirt, its neck stuck out and its label no longer legible. She realized the clearing ahead was larger than she expected.

Was this the destination Leyda had mentioned? Deep in the woods, farther than most hunters would dare to tread, it seemed the perfect place for werewolves to make their home.

The noonday sun shone through the trees and the wind picked up. Mercy tried to brace herself. She had never met werewolves in the wild during the day. Would they be living as animals? Or like humans?

She had no idea what to expect.

———

AS THE PATH TURNED to a soft moss, Mercy couldn't suppress a gasp. Of all the things she had expected, she never thought there would be so much blood.

Great red blotches spilled in puddles on the forest floor. Bloody handprints clung to the trunks of trees and trails of blood extended out in all directions from their small path. It couldn't have possibly been done by one werewolf, but many. Clouds of flies clung to the areas like an oasis. The blood smelled old, as though it had sat there for days under the bright sun. Mercy put the back of her hand to her nose to help block out the scent.

No wonder they had to make camp so far away from Kanta. Any dog would smell it if they lived any closer. What a horrible way to live. It had to be done from the prey the group dragged back to the campsite every night. That was the only reason she could think of.

"Are these—is all this blood from their victims?"

Leyda shook her head. "No, not their victims, child. The transformation to and from a wolfish form every night is not a clean, pretty sight. It is messy and grotesque. This is the blood of those who live here, the blood of the werewolves, the blood of your fellow Kantans. The hunters back in Kanta think the beast itself is the monster, but we know better. The monster is in the disease. Thomas understands that now. Hopefully you will too."

She glanced at Leyda in confusion at that last remark, but before she could ask what she meant, gun shots rang through the air. Mercy jumped and cried out, resisting the instinct to flee back into the woods. Leyda dropped to the ground and Mercy followed her example, shaking from head to toe.

Another shot rang off, closer this time. Mercy jumped again and put her head down into a clean patch of fresh-smelling moss as she covered her head. Her heart pounded in her chest. This couldn't be normal. Had something happened to them? Was something wrong? Mercy swallowed down the panic, half expecting Mitchell to come running toward her or to hear Carter calling for her deep in the woods, but that wasn't possible any longer. They were gone. She had to stay focused, stay present, and not be caught up in her terror from the past.

"Stop wasting ammunition, you idiots!" Leyda cried. "It's Leyda! I brought a friend, but this is a terrible way to greet her!"

The silence stretched for far too long and Mercy consciously tried to slow her breathing to listen and to learn.

"She smells like a human!" A man called back and Mercy clenched her teeth. She thought of Leyda's words earlier: a sheep entering a wolf's den. She thought Leyda was merely being melodramatic earlier, but now she knew better.

"That's because she is a human!" Leyda got to her

feet, her hands balled into fists at her sides. "Now quit firing at us, or I'll snap that rifle in two."

"We're taking precautions." The man grunted in annoyance. "Too many wander out this way these days. Too many people looking for fresh hunting grounds."

Leyda gestured for Mercy to get to her feet. It took a few moments for her to be able to. Her legs wobbled beneath her and her disguise felt unbearably warm. The breeze helped her steady herself. She followed Leyda and they approached several men armed with rifles. They looked like they had barely survived a wild animal attack. A large man with pale skin and red hair gave them a nod. Both of his arms were covered in black and blue bruises. He put the hilt of the gun on the ground with practiced ease. Leyda went up to him and pulled him into a hug.

"It's good to see you again," he said.

"Henry, you look terrible."

Henry shrugged, giving a half smile that didn't meet his eyes. "It's been rough."

She turned to the other guard and put a hand to her mouth. "Oh, Andrei!"

This guard was younger and didn't look much older than Mercy. He had dark brown skin and a bandage wrapped over his left eye.

"What in the world happened?"

Andrei shrugged. "I don't know. I just woke up without it one morning. It doesn't hurt anymore though. I think it might be growing back, so that's good, right?"

Leyda put a hand on his shoulder and spoke to them as though they were her brothers. Both of them looked terrible. They were clearly malnourished, exhausted, and sported bruises and injuries more numerous than Mercy ever expected. Leyda told her that the disease was the true enemy in Kanta. She hadn't fully understood what that meant. Until now.

Father had taught her that werewolves were always vicious, regardless of whether it was day or night. He said the only way they could be gotten rid of was to kill them. At the time, Mercy had believed and agreed with everything he said. It was hard to shrug off the teachings she had once believed completely, but she couldn't deny the facts before her.

The ridiculous amounts of spilled blood on the outskirts of their encampment, the physical abuse she could clearly see on their bodies, and Leyda's insistence that Thomas was her only chance to ever be free of lycanthropy. Regardless of whether Thomas was able to help them or not, Mercy had to admit that the plight these people faced was horrid. Father used to say werewolves were disgusting creatures and they would instantly turn on their friend or family at any moment. To him that proved they were vicious and cruel beasts, nothing more, but Mercy felt a growing remorse for them like she had felt when she first spotted the grinder at the mill and saw the werewolves who were chained to it.

What she had always been taught to believe was simply not true.

Leyda asked, "How is Rose? Is she still with you? Is she safe?"

Henry put a hand on Leyda's shoulder. "She's fine. Don't worry so much."

Andrei looked to Mercy with a curious gaze. "And who is this one?"

Leyda turned as though suddenly remembering Mercy was standing there. Her demeanor changed instantly. "This is Mercy. We rescued her. She's staying with us at the mill now, helping out."

Andrei put a hand out and Mercy shook it. "Good to meet you," she said, not attempting to hide her high-pitched voice.

He grinned. "You too. I've never seen a girl my age before. I didn't think the traffickers allowed them to exist in Kanta for long." He gave a warm grin that made a flush rise in her cheeks. She was grateful for the bandages hiding most of her face.

Before even thinking about whether it was a smart idea or not, she said, "I escaped a pair of trappers with Leyda's help. She helped me and now I'm trying to help her."

Mercy locked eyes with Leyda who looked shocked by her words.

Andrei crossed his arms, looking between the two of them. "She seems honest enough, but can we trust her, Leyda? We've never let humans past the boundary. Is it a good idea?"

"Then make an exception," Leyda countered. "I'm vouching for her. I've already warned her that if she pulls a gun on any of you, I'll rip her throat out. She seemed to take the hint."

Mercy winced.

Henry laughed and shook his head. "What's your name? If you survived coming all the way out here without Leyda killing you, then that's a good enough reason for me to let you pass."

"Mercy Pinkerton," she said with a nod, but both Henry and Andrei exchanged a look.

"Wait a minute. Pinkerton?" Henry said, "As in Solomon Pinkerton? Are you related to him?"

Mercy considered lying but realized that did her no good here. They trusted her into their secret camp and she had to trust them not to judge her family too harshly.

"He was my father. Two werewolf hunters who were actually trying to sell me off gunned him down in the woods. They left me for dead until Leyda and Thomas rescued me."

Henry gaped at her. "He was a ruthless man. I'm surprised they got him like that."

"I grew up training to be a werewolf hunter," she admitted, trembling from head to toe. "But I'm learning the truth. I'm learning what's really been happening here in Kanta all these years and how naïve I was. I want to help. I want to stop all of this and find a way to end this disease. If you want to leave me out here, I can do that. But if you'll trust me, I really would like to help if possible."

Henry didn't look convinced. Maybe he had known her father once, or maybe he had lost friends to her father's work, but there was a hesitance in his gaze that wouldn't leave. Mercy wondered how many others would also be wary of her name like this. She should have called herself the Wolf of Kanta again, that would have at least gotten some laughs.

"I didn't bring her all the way here just to wait on the doorstep," Leyda muttered. "If you want to change perceptions, you can't lock everyone out. That only makes us look more like monsters."

"I like her," Andrei stated. "I say we let her in. What's she going to do? She's just a human."

Henry huffed. "You don't even know the Pinkertons. Her father brought in more of our kind to Thomas than any other hunter in Kanta. And you want to let her waltz in?"

"Sure, why not? She's not her father, Henry. None of us are. Leyda knew the risks bringing her here, and she's vouching for her. Quit being stuck in the past. Solomon is dead like she said—my apologies, by the way. If the traffickers are brazen enough to take him down, then they're tearing our town apart."

Mercy blinked at him. Even though they lived so far out in the woods, exiled and afflicted with a terribly destructive disease, they still considered Kanta to be their home. Even though they might never see it again. It was heartbreaking.

Henry sighed and dragged his fingers through his red hair. "I guess if Leyda is vouching for her, it's fine. You two are way too pushy."

Leyda glanced to him, "That's because we don't have all day. The sun won't be in the sky forever and I need to get Mercy home before it's dark."

Henry's eyes went wide. "Oh! Oh, I'm sorry, Mercy. I didn't even think about that. Of course, you two can come in. Just be mindful of the time. I don't want you to get hurt. Leyda can take care of herself but you—er…"

"Thank you," Mercy said with a smile. "Yes, I know the risks. I've been working around werewolves for weeks, believe it or not."

Henry blinked at her.

"Come on," Andrei said, leading the way. "Let me show you around. Oh, and it might be a good idea not to mention you're a Pinkerton." He lowered his voice, "Not everybody is as easily persuaded as Henry is."

Mercy nodded.

5

THE EXILED

PAST THE MAKESHIFT TENTS and far from the pools of blood, the pack used a clearing as an encampment. People wrapped in clothes full of holes huddled around a roaring campfire in the center of it. Gaunt cheeks and hollow eyes stared at Mercy with suspicion. Everyone looked ill and exhausted. Some had injuries far more grievous than Andrei's bandaged eye, and Mercy shuddered at the realization that such injuries were common for werewolves. Did it come from being attacked by hunters? Or did the transformed werewolves injure themselves trying to get to Kanta, harming themselves trying to reach the powerful scent of humans?

Shelter seemed to be shambled together lean-tos barely standing against the weather and poorly suited for the coming winter. Others had simply spread muddy blankets over bare patches of grass as makeshift beds. As Kanta's people dwindled, the werewolf camp had clearly grown too fast. There wasn't enough space or resources for the amount of people living there.

Every one of them looked exhausted and beaten. Come spring, Mercy wondered how many would still be alive. All eyes were on her as Andrei led her to the center of camp. They looked angry to see a human here.

A short woman approached. She had bronze skin with a scar on her right cheek that gave her face a pinched look. She had long, curly black hair and wore colorful, layered skirts littered with holes. "Leyda?" the short woman whispered, "is that you?"

Leyda stepped forward and pulled the remainder of her face coverings off, fully exposing her head.

"It's me, Rose," Leyda whispered, her voice thick.

Rose ran forward and flung her arms around Leyda's neck, planting kiss after kiss on her face, her neck, and her lips.

"It's been forever! I feared I would never see you again after you left last time." She pulled away and examined Leyda's face, turning her chin left and right. "You're farther along than last time," she whispered and tears came to her eyes. "But you're definitely not human." She frowned.

Leyda barked a bitter laugh. "You and I both know I'll never be fully human again. Doesn't matter what I look like."

Rose grinned as tears streamed down her cheeks, and pulled Leyda into another hug, holding so tight it seemed she might never let go. Finally Leyda freed herself and turned to the small gathering that had formed at their arrival. There must have been twenty or thirty in total.

"I assure you that my human friend here, Mercy, is not here to hurt anyone. She is here to help."

Mercy felt her face flush as all eyes turned to her. She hadn't expected such a comment from Leyda, not after their arguments in the forest.

"The man who is helping me to slowly become human is looking for a cure to the disease that affects all of us."

Many scoffed as she said this. A few turned back to the fire, muttering under their breath. Mercy only caught a few phrases.

"She is clearly delusional…"

"Who would want to work with that Butcher Thomas?"

"She's still not cured. And look at her!"

"…even more of a monster than we are."

Mercy gaped at them. Here was Leyda, a living, breathing example of the good that Thomas's research could do, but they couldn't see it. Sure, it wasn't perfect, and Thomas himself admitted he felt overwhelmed by the challenge, but there was clear promise. Leyda was no longer a werewolf even if she wasn't completely human either. Mercy admitted Leyda didn't look wonderful, but anything was better than transforming into a werewolf every night. Couldn't they see the hope standing right in front of them?

She regretted mentioning her doubts in Thomas's work to Leyda earlier. She had no idea the promise the research had until she saw the way the werewolves had to live in the camp. For some reason she had expected them to be living like anyone else, in houses, maybe even on farms, but not this. Leyda was right to put her hope into him, even if it would be years before a true cure came, even if a cure never came. It was still better than this torture every night.

"I can't believe you brought along someone so young." An older woman glared at Leyda. "Even if she did get sent by that monster, Farrell. It's too dangerous bringing a human out here."

Leyda lifted her chin in defiance. "If we hope to be fully human again, then we need to have the trust of humans. We need to have humans on our side if we ever hope to return to living with them. They are frail creatures compared to us, and it's important to remember that."

Mercy stared at her. Was that the real intention Leyda had brought her? She wanted to remind them what it was like to be around a weak human? She couldn't help but feel insulted, but then again, the statement was true. She was easily outnumbered. The realization made the hair stand up on the back of her neck.

The old woman looked Mercy up and down, raising her eyebrows in clear disgust. "Not every human is as frail as this one. I was a tough old broad once."

"Come on, Beatrice." Leyda snarled. "Be nice."

Mercy cleared her throat and pushed away her pride before asking, "When was the last time you were around a human?"

Beatrice looked up at her, as though seeing her as a person for the first time. "A living human? A few years, I imagine." She let out a long breath. "Too long, I suppose."

To Mercy's surprise, Leyda gave her a nod and a small smile. Was that encouragement? Was Mercy actually doing well and impressing Leyda? Twice in one day, it was practically a record. So Mercy was here to be an example, to remind them of her humanity.

"So you came all the way out here to walk straight into a werewolf camp?" Beatrice asked with a tick of a smirk at the corner of her mouth. "Brave or stupid?"

"I hope brave, but probably stupid," she admitted.

Andrei approached from the side, wearing a ridiculous grin on his face. He didn't have his rifle anymore, which she appreciated. Of all the werewolves from the camp, he was the only one who seemed comfortable approaching her, and she wasn't sure what that meant.

He snorted. "Yeah, I lean toward brave. I wouldn't want your job, disguising yourselves and wandering those woods, that's for sure. Not with all those hunters roaming about."

"It was more of an assignment than a job. We couldn't get spotted, so Leyda did this." She gestured to her clothes.

"You both look a lot like hunters. It's a good disguise."

Beatrice rolled her eyes and turned back to the fire.

Andrei put a hand out. "Sorry I didn't introduce myself earlier. My name is Andrei. Can we try this again —without guns this time?"

Mercy shook his hand, noticing his pointed nails. He must have noticed because he pulled his hand back and shoved both hands into his pockets.

"Sorry," she muttered. "I've only met transformed

werewolves before, or partial ones like Leyda. I don't mean to stare."

"You're fine," he muttered. "I can't remember the last time I saw a human when I wasn't, you know… Hey, are you hungry? I could fry up some fish real quick."

Mercy's stomach growled before she could decide how to reply. How long were they planning to stay? She looked for Leyda to try to get an idea, but she had disappeared with Rose.

"I heard that." Andrei snickered. "Come sit with me and I'll put something together."

Mercy followed him around the roaring fire. At least twelve people huddled under blankets near it, speaking in low whispers as they passed. It was getting chilly as the day progressed but it wasn't that cold. It was strange they were all so cold. Then again, they transformed every night and if the puddles at the edge of the camp were any indication, they lost a lot of blood in the process. Beatrice coughed, then it worsened into a loud hacking. It was so bad she sounded like she might suffocate for a moment. Several people stared at her, but none of them went to help. A weird silence fell over the camp. Finally Beatrice recovered and caught her breath. Someone rubbed her back, and the noise of the camp resumed.

Mercy sensed no urgency, no worry, just a dreaded waiting, an expectation. Illness had to be common judging from the state of the camp, but did that also mean death was too? A reluctant acceptance permeated the camp, a cold chill that wouldn't thaw regardless of how many logs were tossed on the fire. Death hung in the air like circling vultures. That was why so many scoffed at Leyda's talk. They had already resigned themselves to their fates. They had given up on living and now waited for death's inevitable visit. Mercy was horrified.

They weren't monsters like her father had always said, they were sick. They had a terrible disease and needed help, not silver bullets. In that moment she understood why Thomas took sympathy on Leyda even though she had taken both of his arms. She understood why he kept all the werewolves in his lab who had gained their minds. She understood why Leyda took the long, dangerous trek out here to visit. She too felt sorry for them.

"Here we go." With a grin, Andrei turned and gestured to a bare patch of dirt near the fire. Mercy was pulled from her thoughts.

"Thanks," she muttered and let Andrei take her hand as she sat down around the campfire, feeling the eyes of every other werewolf on her.

<hr>

THE FISH SMELLED DELICIOUS, but Mercy was surprised by all the flies that appeared as Andrei cooked it for her. One minute there were none. The next minute a dozen of them buzzed around the food despite the flames. She swatted at them without much luck.

"Why are there so many of them?"

"It's all the blood, I think," Andrei said with a rueful

sigh. "We make more puddles every night and it doesn't rain enough to get rid of it all. So the flies love us." He shot her a smile that was supposed to be reassuring, but he just looked sad. "At least someone around here likes us, right?"

Mercy shook her head. "That has to be painful."

"Yeah…" He flipped the fish to the other side. "By the way, you're going to have to take off that wrapping if you want to eat anything." He gave her a smug expression and Mercy rolled her eyes.

"I don't need my whole face to eat."

His smile fell. "But I want to know what you look like under there. That's not fair."

She shook her head. "If I can't put these wrappings on right, I'll be in big trouble when we head back to Kanta. I barely escaped the traffickers last time, and I don't want to try my luck again."

Andrei gave a solemn nod as he scraped the fish onto a wooden plate. "That honestly sounds terrifying. At least werewolf hunters just want to kill us. I can't imagine what that had to be like. You're not even sick like us." A hollowness came to his eyes. It reflected the despair she saw in the others and made her uncomfortable. He gave her the plate of food. "We don't have silverware, so wait until it cools off first." He sat down beside her, linking his arms around his knees, staring at the fire.

"I guess I'll have to remind everyone how to use a fork once they're cured."

That made him laugh.

Mercy picked at her food, listening as Andrei

explained why the camp was short on luxury. Silverware was easy to bend and break. The cast iron skillets were far more durable, and the wooden plates weren't too hard to replace. Werewolves had a bad habit of breaking things when they transformed, so glassware was out of the question. If it wasn't durable, it wouldn't last, which was why people wore layers of clothes to stay warm and why they lived in lean-tos that could be repaired each morning instead of a house that could take a long time to rebuild.

"Thomas Farrell is trying to create a cure," she said. "He made progress watching one man transform into a werewolf, but now he needs someone to volunteer to be a guinea pig."

Andrei bit his lip as she spoke and his leg shook. "Leyda was his guinea pig before. Why can't she do it again?"

"I don't know, maybe because she's halfway through? I imagine that might mess up his experiment."

He grinned and Mercy felt warmer when she saw that smile. Or maybe it was just the campfire. "You say that as if you know what his experiment is about."

She put her plate aside. "I help take care of his lab. I care for the werewolves who have their minds, the ones in cages in his laboratory."

"Do they transform every night like we do?"

"No, they're always werewolves, but their minds are human. So I have to take care of them."

Andrei's leg bounced more at her words. "Lucky devils," he said with a grin.

"What do you mean?"

"They get to see you every day."

Mercy blushed red hot so she was very glad she still wore her face coverings and Andrei couldn't see it.

"It's different for guys," she said far too quickly. "The Liquid Lead makes them lose their minds for good, but for women it—"

He held up a hand. "Yeah, I know all that. Leyda told us the first time she visited after she got her awesome metal arms. But if Thomas comes through on his promise and his research works, I might be able to be human again, or at least some form of human. To be honest, it sounds better than what I've got now."

"And if it doesn't work—"

"Then I don't have to worry about doing guard duty every day, or worry about getting killed by a hunter every night, or that I could keel over in front of the campfire come winter like most of the pack. It honestly sounds like a sweet deal."

Mercy stared at him in disbelief. "But...you could throw your life away."

He flung his arms out. "I'm a werewolf, Mercy. I've already thrown my life away. My parents are gone, my brother and sisters are gone, and my family here..." He shook his head and lowered his voice. "All of them are just waiting to die at this point. Like they've already given up. I'm not like them. I want to do more than fetch water and wield a damn gun." He locked eyes with her, his eyes bright with excitement. "You two came here looking for someone to volunteer, and I think I'm the best option you have."

Mercy winced at his words. "You don't understand.

You haven't seen the grinders or what the werewolves pulling them look like, especially toward the end. If Thomas makes a mistake, that would be your fate. You would practically be dead."

He shrugged and pushed his arms behind him as he leaned back. "It's a better death than dying here." He gave her a rueful smile. "Besides, I can't ask you out on a date if I'm a werewolf. If I can't ask a pretty girl out, then really what's the point of living?"

Mercy narrowed her eyes at him. "I'm sorry, but please tell me there's more logic to your decision than that."

He snorted and Mercy had the urge to smack him. Instead her attention was pulled away by Leyda's outraged voice.

"I refuse to accept no as an answer," she cried, pushing her way out through the fabric curtain of one of the lean-tos. Rose followed close after her, clearly upset.

"I'm sorry I'm not as brave as you are." Rose's voice wavered as she spoke. Her cheeks were wet and her eyes red as she wrung her hands together.

"I came all this way to make sure you were safe, to find a way for us to be together. And now you refuse to come with me."

Rose took Leyda's hand. "I have a place here. I have family here. Even if this miracle cure did work, I would leave all of my friends behind. I can't do that."

"What about me? Don't I count?"

Rose wrapped an arm around her waist. "Of course you count. But we can't live together any longer. Your life would be in danger every night and I can't allow you to risk that."

"First of all, it's my life, and I'll do what I want with it." Leyda wrenched free of Rose's arm. "Second, you wouldn't be roaming about every night transformed. Did you not hear any of what I proposed? You could be a half-creature like me, if it didn't work. That would be the worst that could happen. And if it did work, then you would be cured and I would be the monster."

Winding her hands into her skirts, Rose kept her eyes downcast. "I would rather die as a werewolf than live in a half form like that."

Mercy winced. Beside her, Andrei sucked in a breath.

Leyda's eyes went wide and she backed away as though physically hurt. Barely able to speak, Leyda sputtered, "You—you would rather—live like *this*?" She gestured to the entirety of the camp, undoubtedly to draw attention to the filth and sickness of it.

A hush came over the encampment as all eyes turned to Leyda. It was one thing to suffer in such conditions, but it was very different when someone pointed it out with such obvious disgust.

Eyeing Rose, Leyda, and the crowd of onlookers that surrounded them, Mercy easily could see where this was headed. Leyda was walking on thin ice, so wrapped up in her argument with Rose that she didn't even notice the shift among the others. Leyda might be strong on her own, but against the entire werewolf pack? She wouldn't stand a chance. It didn't matter if Leyda was once part of their pack, she was no longer considered family like she once had been. She was making a bad scene. If she didn't watch what she said, she might not ever be allowed back.

Mercy never used to interrupt her father when he was about to put his foot in his mouth. She used to let him do it and let him suffer the consequences, even if that meant he unloaded his rage on her later. One time he made an insulting joke to Dr. Keene who was visiting and was reprimanded for it for hours after. It was funny for Mercy at the time because usually she got in trouble for just about anything, and it was great to see her father put in his place. Of course, he never wanted to speak of it again.

But there was nothing funny about this. As the disapproving silence extended, Mercy feared they would get chased out of the camp. So she did the only thing she knew, she got to her feet and spoke up.

"I think we need to leave now." She approached the two women. Leyda looked up at her as though about to spit an insult, but Mercy added, "I think we've worn out our welcome here."

"Hmph, worn out our welcome? These are my people. This is my family!"

The silence that followed said more than any words could. None of them stood up for her, not even Rose who backed away from her. She looked at Leyda as though ready to burst into tears.

Mercy took hold of Leyda's sleeve and tugged her toward the entrance. Leyda could have fought her, but she didn't. Mercy had expected her to. Maybe she finally had noticed the outrage all around her. Maybe she finally understood she didn't belong like she once did. Whatever the pack used to be for her, it was no longer that.

Henry stood waiting for them near the path, an apologetic expression on his face. "Things are different now is all. You've been gone a long time, Leyda."

Leyda wrapped her face up with practiced ease, tossing fabric around in clear agitation. "When I lived here, we bemoaned the loss of our humanity. Now it looks like you're all just sitting around waiting to die."

Henry shrugged. "I guess we've come to terms with our fate and what we are. It sounds like you're still trying to figure that part out."

Leyda leaned toward him and gripped his shoulder. "Is this truly the legacy you want to leave? Protecting people who don't want your protection?"

Henry blinked and gaped at her in confusion.

She stepped back and swung the final swath of fabric over her mouth, making the rage in her eyes all the more apparent. "I have a home and I know what I am deep down even if my flesh doesn't reveal it." She turned back to the onlookers in the camp. All eyes were still on them. "I thought I had friends here, a family to call my own, but I was wrong."

Her gaze lingered on Rose for a long moment before she turned and stomped into the forest.

Mercy turned briefly to Henry. "Thanks for having us. I'm sorry—for all of this."

It was weak and she knew it, but she had no better words or even an excuse for Leyda's behavior. Unlike Leyda, she didn't have the luxury of losing her temper whenever she wanted. Any of the werewolves in that clearing could have killed her and she knew that. She hurried to Leyda's side, trying not to trip on the roots and brambles.

"I don't know why I even try!" Leyda spat. "Apparently they just want to die as the beasts they are."

"Well that's not very nice," a familiar voice said from behind them.

They both turned to see Andrei trailing behind, hurrying to catch up.

"Andrei, what are you doing here?" Mercy asked.

He gave her a sheepish grin. "You said you needed a volunteer and since Rose wasn't interested, I figured I'd step up."

Leyda glared at Mercy.

"I told him the risks," Mercy said gesturing to him. "I told him that if it failed he would lose his mind for good. I didn't actually think he would come."

Mercy tried to feel more concerned and worried for him, but truth be told she was actually very glad to see him. It would make the long trek back to the mill more bearable and, if she was being completely honest with herself, she liked seeing him smile. He was growing on her and she wasn't sure what to make of it.

Andrei jutted a thumb over his shoulder. "Have you seen what the pack has turned into? A bunch of grumpy werewolves sitting around the campfire, reminiscing about the past and doing nothing for the future, ignoring the obvious escape hatch that opened up right in front of them." He shook his head. "There's no future for me back there. As the youngest, I'd have to take care of everybody until their bodies wore out from the change. I've seen enough death. Who would want to live like that? I don't care if your kooky friend knows what he's doing or not. Anything is better than living and dying like that."

Leyda turned to Mercy with a sneer. "Is there truly no one else you think would be willing to try?" She sounded more sad than angry.

"I didn't think you all could be choosy about this," Andrei said with a nervous laugh.

"You're young. Too young to understand what you could lose here," Leyda stated.

"I think I have a pretty good idea. The only other person you might be able to get someday is Henry, but you couldn't drag him away right now. With me gone, he's the only one on guard duty until someone else volunteers. And he may not approve of everything they do, but he wouldn't leave them without protection. He's stubborn to a fault."

Frowning, Leyda stared down the path toward the camp. "I had no idea it had changed so much. It's like they've lost all sight of hope."

"Turning into a monster every night will do that to you. People disappear, could be dead or captured, who knows. People die from the stress of the change. It's brutal, Leyda, you've been there. You know that. I know I haven't been a werewolf long, only a couple of years, but I've seen how it wears folks down. Some people can't take it."

She nodded and took a deep breath. "I guess we need to get moving so we can beat nightfall."

Mercy glanced up to see the sun had hovering near the tops of the trees. Her heart skipped a beat. She hadn't realized they had stayed for so long. Of course the encampment was so far from Kanta that staying for merely a few hours felt like too long compared to the long walk back.

She voiced her fears aloud. "Do you think we'll make it back in time?"

"It's a straight shot, so we should. Keep up, you two. We don't have the luxury of a leisurely stroll."

A cold wind tore through the trees and Mercy picked up the pace.

6

———————

THE DISEASE

A QUICK PACE meant all three were panting as Leyda, Andrei, and Mercy jogged back to Kanta. The underbrush was unforgiving and all the while Mercy watched the sun dip further into the trees. By the time she could make out the great monolith of Farrell Mill in the distance, the sun just touched the horizon. They were all exhausted, but getting to Kanta was only the first challenge.

Leyda paused to catch her breath, one hand on her hip and another massaging her side. The wind had turned cold as night crept closer, but Mercy was still covered in a sheen of sweat.

Andrei was clearly worried, but he didn't complain once about Leyda's commands or the quick pace. In the dwindling sunlight on the edge of town, Mercy could see all the bloodstains, all the holes, all the clear claw marks in the clothes he wore. If she had believed him when he offered to volunteer earlier, they might have been able to find better clothes for him at camp.

"Wow, it's bigger than I remember!" Andrei said. "Even the mill has grown."

Mercy turned to Leyda. "I'm worried he's going to be an obvious red flag if we take him by the jailhouse and Mr. Pillsby sees him."

Leyda looked at her in confusion, then to Andrei and sighed. She hadn't taken his appearance into consideration either. Both she and Mercy were too distracted when they left the camp. Leyda from her fight with Rose, and Mercy...well, she was distracted by Andrei, far more than she should have been. Now his life might be in danger due to her own foolishness. How Dad would shake his head at her if he was alive, getting her head turned around by a boy of all things.

"What if we took him down by the General Store?" Mercy asked. "We could avoid the jailhouse completely. It might mean cutting through the bushes to get to the mill, but it might work."

Andrei shook his head. "Too dangerous. I've only been a werewolf for a couple of years and I used to work down at the store. I don't like the thought of somebody recognizing me. I mean, I look like a werewolf." He chuckled. "But even if they didn't know that, they might ask me inside for a bite to eat or something, I don't know."

Mercy and Leyda exchanged a look. Neither of them had prepared for this, but there was a lot they hadn't prepared for.

"Maybe I could give him my disguise," Mercy said. "Then you take him down, get him locked up, then come back to get me."

Leyda's eyes went wide. "That's not a good idea. You should take him. You're too much of a target out here."

Ignoring her, Mercy was already removing her disguise. "Nope, it has to be you. If Thomas closed the laboratory door, you're the only one who can open it. Remember? You've got to get him in a cage."

Leyda clenched her fist. "Damn you, Thomas. You and your ridiculous security system."

Mercy removed her wrappings around her face and chest and turned to hand them to Andrei. He was distracted, watching the sun slowly set in the distance, so she had to shove them into his chest for him to notice.

"Oh! Thank you, I don't—" He froze when he made eye contact with her, the words lost on his lips.

"You better quit staring and put those on already."

He blinked. "Uh yeah, okay." He started getting the wrappings on, but he kept staring at her. "You're so pretty, I didn't realize…"

Mercy felt her cheeks burn and she grunted in annoyance. Leyda went over and started wrapping up Andrei's head as angrily as she could until Andrei was a pair of shocked eyes staring out from a sea of cloth.

"Keep your hormones under control, kid." Leyda snarled. "And keep up. I need to get you into a cage and get back so your girlfriend doesn't get eaten."

"Girlfriend!" Mercy cried.

Leyda's eyes crinkled with amusement, then she grabbed Andrei's hand and dragged him toward Kanta.

"Be careful!" Andrei called to her as Leyda yanked his arm, berating him for drawing attention to them.

Mercy couldn't help but smile as they left. Despite

how foolish he could be sometimes, she really liked him. She took a deep breath of the crisp evening air and reminded herself that regardless of how much she liked him or how he made her feel, he was a werewolf and she was a human. In a few minutes he would eat her as soon as look at her. She thought of Rose back at the werewolf camp. She had said she and Leyda couldn't be together since they were so different now. She and Andrei had a similar dilemma. She hoped his mind would survive the experimental formula Thomas was going to give him even though deep in her heart she knew exactly how it would work. He would be no better off than Carter soon. And then she would never see his smile again…

No, she didn't need to go down that road. Not yet.

Taking a deep breath, she leaned against a tree and waited for Leyda to return. She watched as the sun sank further into the horizon. With every minute that passed, Mercy felt her worry grow. The air grew colder and the wind raked through the trees. When the stars started twinkling overhead, that's when she began to panic.

It didn't take that long to take someone down to the laboratory. She knew the route by heart. Did Andrei have second thoughts once he heard the grinders and smelled the blood in the air? Did he fight Leyda when they got to the mill? That honestly didn't sound like him. He knew better than most what he was getting into. Did they run into trouble at the jailhouse? She thought of Jacob Pillsby eyeing them as they entered into town. Last time he tried to pull Leyda in there, she nearly had passed out from the smell. Andrei probably wouldn't fare much better. If they both passed out and got discovered... a chill went down her spine at the thought.

The purple sky slowly faded to black and Mercy knew she didn't have time to wait any longer. She had to head into town even though she had no disguise. She was not only an obvious girl now, she would also be clearly seen as Mercy Pinkerton for any who had seen her in town before. She didn't have a choice. Either she entered Kanta and took her chances with the human traffickers who lurked there, or she waited in the woods for the werewolves to devour her.

She would take her chances in Kanta. It was the only real option. Shivering as she pushed off the tree, she started downhill into town, keeping her hand close to her gun—grateful that she had brought it.

DESPITE HIS MANY FLAWS, Dad had taught her a good deal about survival. She would be forever grateful to him for that, despite how difficult a person he had been sometimes.

She strained her senses into the darkness as she stepped out onto the dirt street of Kanta. It was empty, which was normal in a town that faced nightly werewolf assaults. No windows were lit, to prevent the creatures from knowing anyone was inside. Having worked beside werewolves now for the past few months, she knew that did little good. Their senses of smell and hearing were too good to be fooled by such simple maneuvers, but it made people feel safe.

Mercy walked down the empty street, trying to calm her own rapid breaths, looking everywhere at once, and listening for any sound that could be a padded footfall on the ground. She knew the woods surrounding Kanta fairly well, and she knew most of the places in the mill, but she didn't know the streets of Kanta. Dad had only brought her here once, and she hadn't had time to explore. Every alleyway she passed meant a potential for ambush and she looked for glowing eyes within every bush. If any werewolves had snuck into town, they had easily a thousand places to hide, and Mercy could only see a hundred. For the first time she felt the oppressiveness of the town, how isolated it felt at night, and she understood what her parents must have felt when they dealt with the onslaught of werewolves every night.

She passed by the inn. Most of the shutters were closed up and she only saw the occasional flicker of candlelight inside. It looked abandoned at night in the ghostly moonlight.

As she approached the jailhouse, she watched the front door, looking for Jacob Pillsby's face to appear. If Leyda and Andrei were found out, would they be killed on the spot or would they be kept in cages? She studied the ground, alert for any sign of a struggle or bloodshed, but she didn't see anything in the area's limited light. Faint footfalls sounded from behind, so faint a blast of wind would have erased it. Mercy spun around as her heart pounded in her chest, but the road was still empty. She looked all along the road, scrutinizing the bushes, the trees, even along the walls of the pub up ahead. But she saw nothing.

Swallowing down her fear once more, she pulled her gun out of the holster and kept it close to her body. She took off the safety. Her hands shook and she willed them to be still. She had to keep her head. Her father had been killed by a gun like this, her mind reminded her, but she pushed the thought away. If there was a werewolf, she needed to protect herself. If it was a human, she didn't want to accidentally kill someone from jumpy nerves. She took a few calming breaths until her hands stopped shaking. Only then did she continue. Her footsteps sounded too loud despite her best efforts to be silent.

A snap like a cracking bone made her jump. In a shadowy corner by the pub, she spotted the hulking form of a werewolf. Crouched over something, it was clearly eating. Mercy grimaced. She glanced toward the shadowy shape of the mill in the distance, then back to the werewolf. Normally she would take cover in another building, but then she could be targeted by a trafficker. The only way she could reach the mill was by passing the werewolf.

She had to hope it was too occupied by its meal to notice her. How food motivated were they with a fresh kill? She had no idea.

Slowly she stepped down the street, trying to look everywhere at once, just in case other werewolves had been drawn by the kill and lurked in the shadows. She thought of the werewolf pack. Did they hunt in packs or were they solitary hunters? Her father always said they hunted alone, but he really knew so little and most of his information had been wrong. She already knew so much more than he had.

Heartbeat pounding in her ears and a cold wind growing, Mercy was directly opposite the creature when she got a clear view of its meal. The man was slumped back against a pile of boxes. A shotgun lay on the ground not too far from his hand. He might have looked to be only dozing, if his insides weren't strewn all around the alleyway and up the wooden boards of the pub wall. Then she saw the man's face and gasped.

Jacob Pillsby's eyes stared up at the empty sky, mouth open and frozen in a silent scream.

A horrible possibility occurred to her: the werewolf could be Andrei.

Maybe Leyda didn't get him back to the mill in time. Maybe Jacob delayed them for questioning, and Andrei transformed and killed him.

The red, tear-filled eyes of Rose came to her then. Maybe she had changed her mind. Maybe she decided to follow them and planned to make it up to Leyda later, but ran out of daylight.

Either way, the gun in Mercy's hands felt heavier now. This time she likely knew the person beneath the fur and claws. She had probably seen them just a few hours ago huddling near the campfire for warmth. Only a few hours was all it took to go from a friendly face at a campsite to eating Mr. Pillsby's guts behind the pub. It was hard to even wrap her head around. It was hard to make sense of any of it.

Finally Mercy got her feet moving again. She was

almost out of sight of the grisly carnage, and began to relax because she smelled the steam from the mill. That meant she was close to safety.

No, wait…the wind carried the scent from the mill. She only started smelling it as the wind kicked up. That meant the werewolf was downwind.

The sounds of snapping bones stopped and a great brown head poked out around the wall of the pub. Glowing red eyes locked onto her. When it growled, she felt it in her intestines.

Her instincts told her to run. Her legs quivered, ready to lunge for the mill. She was close—but was she close enough? She didn't think so. She had seen how fast these creatures could run, not to mention how far they could leap. She still had scars on her back from the werewolf who clawed her that night with her father. His words came back to her as crisp as the day he had said them.

Never run from a werewolf unless you want them to follow. You won't outrun them.

The last thing she wanted to do was provoke a chase. She might as well be dead right beside Jacob at that rate. Swallowing down the dry patch in her throat, she reminded herself to keep breathing, and backed away from the creature with her gun raised.

One step, two steps. The werewolf growled again and it triggered her primal urge to flee. But Mercy refused. Running was death, she reminded herself. Her father hadn't sacrificed his life for her just so she could throw away all his teachings and die. She had too much left to do, too much to learn. Even if it was Andrei, she chose her life over his. Realizing that made her instantly feel horrible…but she knew it was true.

Three steps, four steps. The werewolf put a paw down on the dirt road. It was massive and the claws were coated in blood. She shook her head in warning, even though she knew it was futile. The gun rattled in her hands.

In a flash of a second, the werewolf lunged toward her. Mercy's breath caught in her throat. It moved so much faster than she remembered. Its bloody mouth gaped at her and its arms went out wide.

Mercy's breath came in hot puffs of air. Her trembling fingers squeezed the trigger.

"I am so sorry, Andrei. Please forgive me," she murmured as the gun blasted through the cold night air. The recoil was stronger than she had expected and her arms were thrown back. Pain flared in her shoulders, but the werewolf was flung back too.

It fell limp to the ground. Bloody fur matted its chest from the shot and it whimpered once before curling into a heap. A cold wind swept down the street, bringing with it the smell of steam from the mill.

Hot tears streamed down Mercy's cheeks. Letting the cold air fill her lungs, her eyes flicked to the buildings around her, waiting for other movement, but there was nothing. Nobody cared that a gunshot went off outside. Nobody cracked open a door or peeked out through the shutters. It was just another night in Kanta and the people didn't care about the dead werewolf bleeding out in the street, or Jacob who was a mess beside the pub. Her training told her to keep moving. Other werewolves would be drawn by the scent of blood, but she had to see. She needed to see…to know.

Who she killed.

The claws were the first to retract, then the snout diminished, and the hind legs reformed. Mercy wiped at her cheeks and backed away, putting distance between herself and the werewolf that now looked like a bloody human. Finally the werewolf was gone, and only the naked, bloody body of Henry remained. His dark blond hair was plastered to his head and the blood of Jacob Pillsby covered his mouth. His chest was blasted through with a gaping, gory hole. The gunshot had taken a portion of his heart.

Mercy put a hand to her mouth. It wasn't Andrei or Rose. A feeling of relief washed over her, which was immediately followed by guilt. Henry hadn't deserved this. He deserved to be given a cure. He had seemed like a good person. Andrei liked him. Who was he to him? A friend? Maybe even family?

Had Henry followed them wanting to volunteer as well? Had it taken him longer to get away from the demands of the pack, only to run out of time once he got here?

She swallowed down the tears that threatened to pour out of her. It didn't matter now. Henry was dead and Mercy was the cause. If she hadn't waited so long, maybe he would have lived. Maybe she could have befriended him. As it was, he was just another corpse to wash off the streets of Kanta.

Mercy turned to the great shadow of the mill with a burning rage in her heart. She wasn't sure how she was going to do it, but she was determined to fix this. The disease ravaged Kanta, but it was more than just that. There was so much wrong, so much that needed to be made right. The disease, the town, both had taken so much from her and she wouldn't let them take more.

It had to stop.

PART 2

The Scientist

7

THE MORAL CHOICE

AT ONE TIME Mercy feared being swallowed whole by the behemoth of Farrell Mill, but now she welcomed it. The place felt more like home than her own house had felt living with Dad. There she had felt more like a maid than a member of the household. She had more independence here than she ever did there.

Normally the front gates were wide open during the day, allowing plenty of room for werewolf cages to be brought in. But at night they were closed and the smaller door was the only way inside. She knocked on the door, the metal cold against her knuckles. The door opened a crack and a man appeared. He had scruffy brown hair, pale skin, and a thick mustache. One long scar stretched across his left jaw. She didn't recognize him, but he must be the new guard who replaced Mitchell. She wondered if he knew that Mitchell had been slaughtered on the floor of the tower just a few weeks ago. He narrowed his eyes, probably surprised to see a girl at the door in the middle of the night.

She cleared her throat, but her throat still wavered. "Please, I need to come in. I'm—"

"Please, no names." He held up a gloved hand to stop her, lifting an oil lantern in his other hand to illuminate her. He gave a short nod, his gaze turning hard. "You work here, don't you?"

How did he know that? He had clearly seen her but she had never seen him before. A chill went down her spine, but she nodded.

He pulled the door back so she could enter.

"Thank you," she muttered. She stepped inside and heard him close the door behind her. She didn't stay to chat. The thought of getting to know the new guard that had taken Mitchell's position made her feel icky. He might be a very nice person, the very opposite of Mitchell and Carter, but she couldn't risk it. She needed to put as much distance between herself and him as possible. Besides, she knew where she needed to go.

The waiting room for the werewolves was completely dark and empty. Newly caught werewolves weren't normally accepted until dawn. Through the door and across the metal catwalks above the grinders, her footsteps echoed off the metal in the large empty chambers. Even at night, the grinders turned. The steam was thick in the air and filled her lungs. She dragged her fingers across the cold metal of the railing, feeling places where the paint had flecked off. She leaned over the edge, rested her elbows on the railing, and stared down at the armless werewolves below. All of them had names, backgrounds, families, histories, but none of it would ever be known. They were lost causes now, failed experiments, captured souls lost to the shallow cruelty of Kanta.

She breathed in the thick air and let it back out slowly. She needed to collect herself, to prepare herself. Anxious, she needed to do something but she couldn't figure out what. She knew she had needed to come here to see the grinders, to watch the poor werewolves who ran them, but then what? Her mind swirled with possibilities, questions, horrors, but she struggled to focus on any of it. Her mind was moving so fast she couldn't settle it down and think properly.

She left the catwalk and entered the final building: the tower. The wrought iron circular staircase creaked under her weight as she descended in the dark. The crescent moon gave just enough light through the open windows so she could see her footing. When she stepped off the stairwell, she saw the great metal laboratory door stood wide open. It wasn't even cracked like usual. She swallowed down the nervous twitching of her stomach and stepped through the doorway. Following the path lit by flames from the alcove, she walked down the ramp and entered the laboratory. As soon as she turned the corner she noticed that the once empty cage had been moved. And it was now occupied.

At the back of the room against the far wall, the cage was farther from the entrance. Through the bars, an amber eye stared back at her. Andrei. Somehow Leyda had gotten him into the cage in time. He had lost the wrapping over his lost eye, and all she could see was a sliver of white where his eye was growing back. Ignoring her instincts, she walked closer to him. She needed to be closer to see him fully. Why, she couldn't understand. He snarled and tried to bite the bars. She heard the squeal of his canines against the metal.

Looking at him now, she should have known it wasn't him on the street. She should have remembered his missing eye. Even transformed, the injury was clear. She knew better, but she had panicked.

The closer she drew, the more frenzied Andrei became. As though her very presence drove him mad. She could understand now the terror that her parents had held seeing this kind of reaction every night in the streets of Kanta. The other werewolves crouched down in their cages, whimpering and whining, as they watched Andrei with fear. They had no need to worry. Mercy knew the cages well. It would hold him.

Besides that, now that she saw him in his transformed state, she realized how thin and undernourished Andrei was compared to the other werewolves she saw on a regular basis. He was scrawnier even than the child werewolves in the cages around her.

"Mercy!"

The voice made her jump and she spun around.

Thomas emerged from his office and approached her with a smile on his lips. "Don't get too close. I don't want you hurt." His lazy eye was aimed at Andrei, but his smile began to fade as he drew closer. "What happened?"

She didn't respond. Instead she stared at the boy she thought was cute just an hour or two earlier. His fangs carved indentations in the metal. The other werewolves whimpered with fear from the other cages.

"This needs to stop," she said, her voice cracking. It felt like a dam was about to break, and she wasn't sure what was behind it.

"What?"

"This." She turned and gestured to Andrei, to the other werewolves, to the entire laboratory. "All of it. It needs to stop."

For a moment, Thomas stared at her. At the same time, Andrei began flinging his body against the bars of the cage. Thomas put a hand on Mercy's shoulder, glanced toward Andrei, and then gently urged her ahead of him and into his office.

Mercy didn't resist. He would want an explanation of some kind, but she didn't have one. All she knew was she felt numb, detached, like she was floating through the world. But something was about to come forward, about to break through, and she couldn't put it to words.

He gently pushed her down onto one of his worn, leather chairs and put a thin, ragged blanket over her shoulders. The dinginess of his office matched well with the fur-lined cape he wore. His aesthetic was like a mad royal holed up in his throne room.

When he squatted down in front of her, concern filled his eyes. "Do you want to talk about what happened out there?"

She shook her head.

He steepled his hands together. "Alright, then can you tell me if this is your blood or not?"

That took her a moment to process. "Blood?"

He nodded patiently.

She looked down at herself and realized that she

had blood across her chest and up her neck. "It's not mine." Her voice betrayed her panic.

Thomas pursed his lips and produced a handkerchief. She dabbed at her cheeks and her throat. The redness of the handkerchief when she pulled it away shocked her. Mercy hadn't felt the splatter at the time, but she remembered now that she had shot Henry at very close range. Looking as she did, she was surprised the new guard let her inside at all.

While she cleaned off the blood, Mercy told Thomas what had happened. She spoke about them splitting up at the edge of Kanta, and how quickly night had fallen, and finally her decision to head back alone.

"I'm afraid Leyda and I almost didn't get Andrei into a cage in time. He began to change as we brought him down the ramp. Leyda and I both had to force him in. It was not a pretty sight. She got scratched up badly." Thomas licked his lips. "She's recovering now, but she didn't mention you were still out there. I thought you were in your room."

Mercy closed her eyes. So she had been forgotten. That's why no one showed up. That wasn't like Leyda. Even if they did fight often she wouldn't have left her out there intentionally. She must have been injured bad.

"I'm sorry," Thomas fumbled, tossing the bloody cloth aside. "If I had known—"

"Jacob Pillsby is dead."

Thomas stared at her. "The deputy?"

She felt a pang of pain at that. "Henry is the man I killed. That was his blood on me." She paused as her chest tightened. "He was from the werewolf camp that

Andrei is from. They were friends. I don't know how he's going to react when he—when he finds out I killed him." Hot tears streamed down her cheeks. A ball of ice was thawing inside her chest. "Jacob was a mess. His insides were strewn all across the wall of the pub. I didn't want to kill Henry, but if I didn't, that could have been me next."

The dam broke open and tears streamed down her cheeks. She couldn't speak any longer. Thomas rubbed her back awkwardly, clearly unsure of what to do. He pulled off a spare towel from one of the many shelves, causing glass beakers and metal pipes to shudder. When he pushed it into her hands, Mercy pressed the fabric to her eyes, crying harder than she had since her father died.

When the tears finally subsided, she felt raw.

"I'm sorry that happened to you. I'm sorry she forgot about you. If I didn't have my head in this damn research all the time." He slammed a hand against one of the shelves and one of the empty glass beakers fell over. "Maybe then I would have noticed you were missing!"

She sniffed and shook her head, folding the cloth in her hands. "No, you have to continue your work. You have to find a cure for all of this. It's not just the people who need your help, it's the werewolves too." She took a moment to gather herself and wiped at her eyes. "I think that's why Henry was here. I think he followed us. He wanted to volunteer to help find a cure like Andrei did. He was a good person. Good to a fault." When her voice hitched, Mercy didn't trust herself to continue.

Thomas beamed. "I'm pleased that so many were eager about my research."

She shook her head. "No, they weren't eager. Nobody wanted to come. Andrei just didn't want to die in that camp."

He blinked, clearly thrown off by her words.

Mercy took the advantage to press her position. "We need to stop moving in circles. We need to fix entirely on your research so you can find a cure and these werewolves can have regular lives again."

He gave a small laugh. "But that's what I'm trying to do! I'm so close to finding it, I can almost taste it." He dragged his fingers through his hair. "I feel so close sometimes and yet other times, I feel like I'm at the drawing board all over again."

"When we spoke earlier, you said you weren't sure if you were cut out for this work. Do you still feel that way?"

He took a moment to answer. "I'm…not sure."

She nodded. "Which is why I want to help."

He shook his head, but she interrupted before he could say more.

"I don't mean feeding werewolves or changing bedding. I don't mean washing the walls of your grinders either. I mean helping, really helping. I want to help you make a cure. I'm tired of losing people to this disease—I'm tired of seeing werewolves rule all aspects of my life."

Thomas studied her. "I don't think your father was killed by werewolves. In fact, if Solomon had faced down werewolves instead of humans, he would probably be alive right now." He gave a short laugh then held up his hand. "Sorry, that was in poor taste. Please forgive me."

Mercy got to her feet so she could look him in the eye. "Mitchell killed my father, but we wouldn't have been in town if we hadn't come to sell you that werewolf. You said yourself that the reason they're able to steal so many women from Kanta is because they can blame their disappearances on the werewolf killings. Half the trouble in this town is caused by the existence of werewolves."

He crossed his arms and stared at the wall. "Gods, he was a monster, wasn't he?"

She stepped around Thomas to get closer, trapping him between her, the chair, and one of his many shelves of supplies. "You have to promise me, Thomas, and this will be the hardest part."

He arched his eyebrows. "You want me to make you a promise? Oh, this is rich. After asking permission to work with me, you now want something else too? You really are so much like your father sometimes it's uncanny."

"I need you to stop buying werewolves for your mill."

He froze. A brief look of guilt passed over his face before fading again. His mouth dropped open but no words came out. Mercy waited for a response. She wasn't going to let him weasel out of this, not this time.

"Oh," he whispered. "That."

"You know it's wrong. I know you do. You wouldn't have taken Leyda in otherwise. And even though you're working on a cure, you're still profiting from them grinding flour in your mill."

He pursed his lips and wrung his hands, clearly unable to find a proper retort.

"The werewolves in the camp called you a butcher. And Leyda says you're a monster just like she is. That's the excuse she makes for you. But I see through you both. I know that isn't what either of you are."

He gave a nervous laugh. "Well, I have been called worse."

She pointed a finger at him. "Don't you dare try to distract away from this. It won't work. Have you considered what will happen when you do come out with a cure? You seem to think they'll be so grateful that the werewolves will flock here to appreciative your generosity. They won't."

Thomas rolled his eyes. "You don't know that. I swear, one visit to a werewolf camp during the day and suddenly you think you can tell me how to do research."

Mercy wanted to smack him because he was being so deliberately dense. "Don't turn this into something it's not. I'm not saying how you should do research. I'm trying to help you. Nobody in that camp wanted to come here. We're lucky we got Andrei. If you use him up on some half thought out drug, then we won't get another one. And if you do find a cure, what's the point of making it if nobody will take it?"

He didn't look at her. Not even his lazy eye rolled in her direction. Surely he wasn't trying to bluff her. Surely he wouldn't try such a thing knowing how blunt her father was. Then a realization struck.

"You've never visited the camp before, have you?" she asked.

He gave a shaky shrug.

"You've never visited any of them?"

He hung his head.

Mercy couldn't believe him. "You mean to tell me that you expect werewolves to willingly allow you to dose them with a cure, but none of them have even met you? The same man who made Liquid Lead, a drug known to turn werewolves into mindless working machines? You dismember their kind here on a regular basis. It makes perfect sense that none of them trust you."

Thomas clenched his jaw tight and looked around. She saw what he saw: the endless array of chemicals and beakers on the shelf. He acted like she wasn't there, but his cheeks were flushed with embarrassment. He clammed up when she confronted him directly. She had to try a different tactic.

He was reacting the same way she used to when her father lost his temper and went off in a rage, breaking things around the house and then expecting Mercy to clean everything up afterward. After a few bruises and nearly getting a wooden bowl chucked at her head, she had learned to keep her head down and go silent. She shut down during that time, for fear of aggravating him and making his rage worse.

Thomas must have learned the same. He had wrapped himself up as small as he could. His arms were wrapped around his waist and his shoulders were hunched. Mercy had cornered him, thinking he was trying to slip out of the conversation, but from his reaction he clearly felt like she had boxed him. He acted like he was afraid of her.

Her breath hitched as she considered what Thomas had said earlier: that she was uncannily like her father. At the time, she thought he meant about her demands, but maybe it was more than that. Maybe he wasn't only talking about her negotiation skills, but also her methods of intimidation.

Revulsion reared up. Never had Mercy wanted to possess her father's cruelty. Never had she wished to learn his ability to intimidate someone who wasn't threatening her life.

Thomas was not her enemy. Yes, he was a terrible person, and yes, he was cruel, but he had risked his life rescuing her in the woods the night after her father had been killed. He had risked it again in his laboratory during Carter's wild shooting spree. He did terrible things, but he had been kind to her. He had helped her when no one else cared if she lived or died. Even Leyda hadn't wanted to save her, not really. Leyda was kinder now, but she still saw Mercy as the daughter of a were-wolf hunter.

Despite his flaws, Thomas did not deserve her rage. She wasn't going to get what she needed without his help. She reached out and put a hand on his upper arm. He flinched and that guilt rose up again in her. She forced herself to fix this. They had real problems to solve.

"Thomas," she pleaded.

Finally he turned to look at her, his lazy eye slow to catch up. In a small voice as though afraid of being too loud, he said, "I thought, or I guess I assumed that they would trust me once they saw how effective it was. Once they saw how brilliant my work was they couldn't possibly resist it." He shook his head and reached up to rub on the fur collar of his cape. "I suppose I was naïve about that."

Mercy chose her words carefully this time. She didn't want him crawling back into his shell again. He needed to be honest with her, to trust her, and that wouldn't happen if she tried to intimidate him. She took a step back and gave him more space. Strange that such a seemingly charismatic and self-assured person could get upset by confrontation, but then again, Mercy didn't know much about him. He had always been referred to as eccentric Thomas Farrell when her father spoke of him. A mad scientist, or a lucky fool. Her father never spoke much about him before he created Liquid Lead. However she got the impression he was considered a rich fool. Someone who inherited his father's mill and lived in luxury. If his reaction was any indication, clearly he had dealt with abusive people before. Regardless, he spoke more freely once she gave him space.

"I considered going once. To the werewolf camp, I mean. I wanted Leyda to take me so I could see if others wanted a partial transformation like she has. I wanted to explain it to them first hand. But Leyda refused. I even told her it would help with my research to assist others with a partial transformation, but she wouldn't have any of it. She said I was so renowned among her kind that they might kill me before I even opened my mouth." He gave a sad laugh. "She certainly is clever. I would be nowhere near as effective in my work without her help."

Mercy gestured to the laboratory door. "What about the other werewolves you have here? Couldn't they have gone through a partial transformation too?"

"The others? Oh no, I'm afraid they're wise to the process. Many of them watched Leyda's process as she gained speech and her current form. None of them are willing to risk it. I fully understand that too. It's not an easy existence. Leyda didn't exactly get a choice in the matter, but she has embraced it since."

With a sigh, Mercy turned and started pacing. She focused on trying to figure out this dilemma. It was easier to deal with than the horror she witnessed earlier. Walking helped her legs not feel tense from the adrenaline rush too. "So what you're saying is that even though you're close to a cure, you don't have anyone other than Leyda who is willing to try it."

"We have Andrei. If he's willing to be a test subject, he'll take a full cure, I bet."

It was encouraging to hear Thomas pouring himself into the exercise as much as she was. They both clearly were good at avoiding their problems to help somebody else. Maybe they had more in common than she realized. Though she wasn't sure if she liked that either.

As a thought came to her, Mercy froze in front of a wall of books. She turned the idea over and over in her mind, to look at it from all angles. It was dangerous. If she went through with it, her life would be changed for good. There would be no going back.

"What is it?" Thomas looked keenly at her, like he

could see the idea on her face along with all the dread and fear that came with it.

She turned to him with a stern expression. "You have a tarnished reputation, right?"

He blinked and put his hand up. "I don't know if tarnished is the right word. I mean that's a little harsh."

Mercy smirked. That kingly cape was definitely there for a reason. She held up her hands to calm him down. "Okay, maybe not with the folks who live in Kanta. I'm sure there are plenty who appreciate all the business you bring into town."

He nodded appreciatively.

"However, the people who live in that camp don't have the best opinion of you, as you know."

"You mean the werewolves."

"No, you can't think of them as werewolves, because once you make a cure, they won't be that any longer. They will be humans."

Thomas gave a slow nod. He was following, but reluctantly.

"They are human right now. Yes, they have a disease, but they're still human."

"Mm, technically they aren't right now. It's night. They're transformed and running around."

Mercy sighed. Pinching the bridge of her nose, she reminded herself not to get angry. "Yes. I mean, you're right, but you get what I'm saying, don't you?"

"Yes, I do. It's a little roundabout, but yes. In the eyes of the *people* who live outside Kanta in the camps, I am probably not the best option to be an ambassador for the cure. However, you think you would be more appropriate?"

She cut a glance at him and Thomas merely arched his eyebrows expectantly. She demanded, "Are you trying to mock me?"

"Not at all! Though you were rather rude earlier so you can't begrudge me a tiny bit of mockery, can you?" He laughed and Mercy regretted feeling bad for him earlier. Even if he was smart, he was absolutely insufferable at times. It was really no wonder he worked so poorly with others. She couldn't let him distract her. She needed to stay focused if she wanted not only to help get the cure made but also adopted at the level needed for Kanta to no longer be littered with death.

She folded her arms and stared grimly at Thomas. "Leyda is the reason we got kicked out of the camp today. She's absolutely useless at negotiations."

He sighed and settled down into the chair Mercy had vacated. All his mirth was lost. "You're right, of course. She's wonderful in a fight, but not the best at being diplomatic, I suppose."

"Regardless of what you do, your reputation is tarnished. You're seen as a monster among them. A butcher."

Thomas winced. "Leyda told me that once before, but I had hoped she had misheard." He clasped his hands before him. "Mercy…you have to understand, before you were born, we didn't know the werewolves were human during the day. We assumed they were monsters the entire time. Some still believe this to be true. Even when a few of them approached Kanta in the old days, we all thought it was a ploy to kill and eat us all. We didn't know they were truly suffering. The belief was that if a person became a werewolf, they were no longer human, but a beast." He shook his head. "I understood the truth when Leyda ripped my arms off that day but chose not to bite me. That was not an animal's revenge, but a human revenge. I knew in that moment something was wrong. That those beliefs were wrong." He hung his head, his crimson hair falling over his shoulders. "I realized then I was a fool for believing all that nonsense, but what choice was there? We were fighting for our lives."

Mercy went over and put a hand on his shoulder. This time he didn't flinch away. "You can't change the past, but you can change things right now."

He looked to her with red-rimmed eyes. "Some nights I can't sleep because I stare at those grinders and wonder if any of those werewolves were people I knew." A tear slid down his cheek and he wiped it away in annoyance. "If I fully admit that the werewolves are human and not beasts, then I have to come to terms with the fact that I've enslaved these people against their will."

Mercy stepped away, trying to decide what to say. "I guess that's something you'll have to come to terms with."

Thomas gave a shuddering breath. "We didn't know they were capable of being human, Mercy."

"That's true. But you know now, don't you?"

He looked at her with wide eyes before taking another shaky breath. "Yes, I guess you're right about that. I suppose I don't have an excuse anymore, do I? By continuing this mill, I'm enslaving my own people."

"Yes, you are, and you know it," Mercy said.

"I'll stop buying them. Any werewolf, male or female."

Mercy narrowed her eyes. "If you do that, they'll all be killed in the woods."

Thomas leaned back in the chair and stared up at the ceiling with weary eyes. "What do you suggest? What do I do to exonerate myself of this…blood I have on my hands?"

"Buy them," Mercy said in a cold voice. "Buy every last one of them, whether they've been given Liquid Lead or not. You buy them and you care for them and feed them until you have a real cure. You take the werewolves from the grinders and you move them to a place where they can recover too."

"…but the grinders…" he whispered. "They're my pride and joy."

Mercy leaned down and thumped on one of his metal arms. "I think you're smart enough to come up with something that doesn't rely on human labor, don't you?"

A clarity came over his face as though someone had just pulled back a curtain. "It would be expensive and everyone will call me mad again, but…" He tapped a finger on his lips. "But they would be talking about me."

He glanced to Mercy with a devious smile on his lips. "I'll need your help in the lab far more. I'll need you to study Andrei, to take notes on his physical performance, especially when you're giving him any doses."

She took a deep breath and tried to quell her fluttering heart at the thought of having to be the one to give a potentially dangerous drug to Andrei. Though not sounding as confident as she wanted, she muttered, "I can do that."

"We'll have some angry werewolf hunters on our hands, but they'll be out of a job soon anyway at this rate. Can you read and write?"

She nodded.

"Good, so I should be able to offload the majority of my lab work to you. In the meantime, I can organize the mill, work on upgrading the grinders to better, autonomous technology, and you can debrief me of your findings as the experiments progress. How does that sound?"

Thomas had found his own energy and excitement again but Mercy was feeling daunted by the amount of work she had agreed to. While she knew it was morally the right move to make, she couldn't help but feel like she had agreed to too much.

"Sure," she nodded, trying her best not to panic.

"Excellent! Mercy, if we play our cards right, we might be able to help a lot of people—and make a profit in the process."

Mercy pursed her lips and tried to feel a shred of the same excitement.

8

RESEARCH

MERCY REALIZED VERY QUICKLY she was woefully unprepared to be a researcher. Though she was a quick learner when it came to cleaning grinder walls and feeding werewolves when she learned that before, when it came to taking detailed observation notes, calculating numbers, and trying to work with something Thomas called chemical compounds, she was practically underwater. She knew how to read pretty well, or at least she thought she could, until she was given the assignment of reviewing Thomas's notes from the past month. It was to help her "catch up," Thomas stated, but if this was a race then Mercy moved at a snail's pace.

Instead of sleeping, she poured over Thomas's notes, trying her best to make sense of them. By the end of the week, she was exhausted, yet still trying to find the motivation to change the bedding for the werewolves. To make it easier, and at Thomas's suggestion, she unlocked the cages and let the werewolves wander around the lab while she worked. Most of them were kind enough, and

Helga, the silver one with the child, even tried to scoop up the old hay to help her out.

"Thanks, Helga," Mercy said through a yawn.

"Hey, aren't you forgetting someone?"

She turned to see Andrei standing in his cage, holding a battered blanket up to cover himself. He had pushed most of the used hay into a corner because it was all bloody from his change the night before.

Mercy's eyes went wide. Other than the blanket, Andrei wasn't wearing a thing. For a moment she stood there gaping openly at him while Andrei grinned sheepishly.

"My clothes are hanging up over there. Can you fetch them for me?"

Finally her brain started moving again and Mercy was keenly aware of just how embarrassing she was behaving. Her cheeks went hot as she forced herself not to look at him, obediently getting his clothes off a hook on the wall. They weren't the worn and dirty clothes filled with holes and stained with blood that he had originally come in. Those had been shredded when he transformed that first night. Thomas hadn't given Mercy the assignment of cleaning that mess up, thankfully, but she had seen the bloody remains in a bucket by the entrance to the laboratory the next day. She suspected they were taken down to the furnace to burn, the same place Mitchell's body had burned. These clothes were bright white, almost blinding, and it seemed a poor choice for a replacement considering the bloody hay pile at Andrei's feet.

Mercy held them out to the bars, keeping her gaze

firmly aimed at the floor. Andrei's fingers brushed against hers as he took them and her stomach dropped.

"Thank you," he said. The rustling of clothes indicated he was getting dressed.

Mercy tried to think of something to say, to apologize for herself, anything to fill the awkward empty silence that filled the space. Andrei couldn't help living in a cage all the time or waking up naked every morning, but she could have had a better reaction. She bit her lips, trying to find something decent to say, but all she could think about was how good he looked without a shirt on.

"There, you can look now. I'm decent."

Mercy looked at him then, but she was unable to keep her eyes from drifting down his body. He looked good in the plain white linen, and she was grateful to be able to think again.

"Sorry, I guess you surprised me," she said.

He gave her a devious smirk. "Well there's more where that came from. I put on a show every night."

She gave an awkward laugh. "I don't think that's the kind of show I'm interested in. I mean, when you transform. I mean—ugh, never mind, I don't know what I mean anymore."

Andrei studied her. "You seem really tired." He put a hand to his chest. "I at least have an excuse in here, but you don't. Don't you get a real bed every night?"

"I'm fine," she lied, trying to stifle a yawn.

"Sure you are. Is that why you mixed the soiled hay in with the clean hay over in Helga's cage?"

She spun around. Sure enough, Helga wasn't

helping to scoop up the old hay, she was trying to change her own bedding since Mercy had done such a poor job.

"Oh no, I'm so sorry!" Mercy rushed over to help her, but Helga snarled in response, lifting a warning paw into the air. Mercy didn't dare get too close. "I was just trying to help."

Helga bared her teeth and Andrei laughed behind her. Mercy turned on him.

"Oh, cut it out! I ought to just leave you in your cage with all that filth."

That made him calm down. "What's wrong? Your private suite not comfortable enough?"

Mercy glared at him. "I may not be the best at this work, but this place is all I have now." She gestured to the bare stone walls of the laboratory, the wandering werewolves, and the rake in her hand.

Andrei's face went serious. "Why are you here anyway? You're not a werewolf like us. You're not one of Thomas's experiments. You mentioned your father got killed, right?"

She couldn't help but wince at his words. It still stung and probably always would. "I'm trying to make a difference, to help…somehow. I want to make up for all the werewolves my father killed and captured over the years. Most of the ones down in the grinders are probably from him. Do you know why? Because I helped him do it." She paused and huffed in frustration.

"Hey look, I'm sorry, I didn't mean—"

Mercy didn't let him finish. "I helped make the darts, I dipped them in Liquid Lead. I kept the house so he could come home and rest. Each of those werewolves he caught or killed were on both of our hands, not just his. If I don't do anything to help, then what good am I? If Thomas finds a cure and we can help people, then it might be some kind of redemption compared to all the horrible things I've helped with."

She sent her rake clattering to the floor. She sank down to join it and brought her knees close. She wanted to cry, wanted her tears to fall, but they wouldn't anymore. It's like she had run out of them. Her father had spent his entire life doing what he thought was right only to have been wrong the entire time. Who else could possibly make it right besides her? Who else had that responsibility?

At the creaking of metal, she looked up. Andrei was settling to the floor of his cage and watching her with a sad expression. He probably thought she was pathetic, sitting curled up in a ball like a child. But she couldn't help it, sometimes it made her feel better. Most of the time it didn't, but sometimes it helped.

"It's hard coming to terms with being wrong," he said. "It's hard to admit it and know what to do from there. I think you're making a good first step even though it's difficult. I admire your bravery."

Mercy scoffed and gripped her knees tighter. "Bravery? You don't even know me."

"Sure I do." He grinned. "You're the rabbit that dared enter a wolves' den. You're the girl with the pretty eyes who would actually talk to me." His amusement faded to admiration. "You're a werewolf hunter who realized she was hunting humans all along and now wants to help them. I don't care what you say, that's brave."

She took a deep breath. Perhaps he was right. It was strange how when she thought about it she felt worse, but when he talked about it she felt better. "Thank you for listening and putting up with me. Everything has moved so fast these past few weeks. I hadn't realized that until now."

"So," he gestured toward her. "Can you let me out of this cage now?"

She laughed. "Was that whole speech just to get me to do my job?" She got to her feet and went over to unlock his cage door.

"No, I just hate seeing pretty women upset."

"I wasn't upset."

He arched his eyebrows and stared at her.

Mercy felt her cheeks flush, but this time she didn't mind it. She unlocked the cage door and he stepped out to stretch. She couldn't help but look at him. If things were different, if she wasn't raised to be a werewolf hunter and Andrei wasn't bitten, perhaps they would have had a chance together. Maybe she would be his girlfriend like Leyda had teased. It wasn't too much of a stretch to imagine, was it? As it was, they could only be friends, she reminded herself, not that it was easy. She wanted to hug him, to wrap her arms around his body and feel the muscles beneath his shirt. Wow, where had that thought come from?

"I appreciate a safe place to change, but I will never get used to being locked up." He popped his back.

A yawn pulled Mercy from her strange thoughts as

the many long nights caught up with her. When she opened her eyes, Andrei was staring at her with concern.

"They have you working a bunch, don't they?"

Mercy shook her head. "It's not their fault. I asked to do it."

He gestured to the room with a grin. "You asked to clean out the werewolf cages? Seems like an odd job to request."

She couldn't help but shake her head. Despite her exhaustion from spinning her wheels on Thomas's notes all week, Andrei's words made her heart lighter. She appreciated that about him. "Thomas assigned me the job, but you're right, that wasn't what I volunteered to do."

"So what are you doing exactly? Being his nurse maid?" When he stepped closer, Mercy's stomach dropped.

She wasn't sure what was going on with her body but she wished it would stop already. Pulling herself together, she said, "I told him he needs to stop using werewolves to power his mill."

Andrei gaped at her.

She swallowed down the urge to leave it at that and somehow found the courage to add, "He's working on turning his mills mechanical like his arms are. While he works on that, I'm supposed to help him with his research. I've been poring over his notes all week but it's all over my head." She tangled her fingers in her hair. "My father taught me how to read, but there are words in Thomas's notes I don't understand. Equations, chemical abbreviations. It's too much. Every time I look at them, they make me feel so stupid. I don't know what I was thinking signing up for this. I'm not a scientist or a researcher. I'm a house cleaner and an apprentice werewolf hunter." She gave a bitter laugh. "I can't even call myself that. I've never captured a werewolf on my own."

Her gaze drifted down to the werewolf she had brought in with her father. Even after weeks of feeding her, cleaning out her cage, and talking to her, she still stayed as far away from Mercy as she could every time Mercy let them out of their cages.

A warm hand gripped her shoulder and she turned to see Andrei standing behind her. Her heartbeat sped up. His warm, caramel eyes bore into her. His cheeks were sprinkled with freckles that made his eyes sparkle. She had to grip her own hair to keep from reaching out and dragging a hand over his cheek. Just friends, she reminded herself, even though that distinction seemed so small now.

"You don't give yourself enough credit," he whispered. His eyes never left hers and her heart did somersaults in her chest. "If you found a way to make Thomas remove slave labor from his mill, that's *huge*. I don't think you understand what a big deal this is."

She shook her head. "You see how flighty Thomas is. If I don't help him with his research and show that progress is being made, he could change his mind completely and there may not be another chance."

Andrei pulled at her arm and she let him extract her hand from her hair. Then he cupped her hand within his. Warmth rose in her cheeks as he intertwined their fingers together. His skin felt coarse and dry, and she realized with some surprise that this was possibly the first time in months that he didn't have to sleep outside—maybe even years.

"You're trying to do too much on your own, but you don't have to. Let me help you. I know I'm not much good at night or in the morning when I pass out, but I am here and willing to help if you'll have me."

She squeezed his hand, then she took his other hand in hers. It felt good to be so close to him. As friends and only friends, of course. Nothing more, not at all. He leaned in closer and Mercy's stomach wound up in knots.

"Before I got bitten, I was an apprentice at an apothecary. I know it wasn't anything official, but I've worked with chemicals before. I'm familiar with the equations and the equipment. I might be able to make sense of things—if you'll let me."

She pulled him closer to her until she could lay her forehead against his chest—if she wanted. "So what you're saying is not only have you been a guard, but also a chemist. I guess I got lucky running into you, didn't I?"

His cheeks flamed, making his into his freckles stand out. "You got to use chemicals when you helped your dad. I only got to play with them in the back room. Not like you. You got to actually use them for something, all they wanted me to do was make perfumes or cleaning supplies, really. Nothing great. But at the time it was exciting!"

He rambled on, sounding as if he was trying to

downplay his own experience. Something about the way his pink lips moved when he was nervous and talked quickly, she found absolutely irresistible. He was still talking as she got up on her toes, leaned in, and pressed her lips against his.

Finally he was silent. He was warm against her. The room disappeared and they were the only two who existed. She breathed in his scent and realized he was holding his breath.

She pulled away and was met with wide eyes. Just friends, she had told herself. That kiss was anything but that. She wished she had more self control, but she was also glad she had given in to her instincts.

"Mercy—" he whispered and she couldn't tell if he was admonishing her or wanting more.

She dragged her fingers through his coarse hair. "You are too adorable, and I couldn't help myself," she admitted. "I'm not fooling myself, I know we can't have anything that can really last, but—"

"Not if we find a cure." His eyes blazed with determination. "If I can be fully human again, we can be together. We won't have to hold back. We could really be together then."

Really be together. Mercy's brain emptied at the thought.

A flash of Henry's bloody body came unbidden to her mind, splayed out on the street, pale and bloody. His death had haunted her nightmares every night for the past week, and now it was seeping into the day too. She shook her head and stepped away from Andrei.

"No, it can't be for us. If we work together on a

cure, then we're doing it to prevent more death…like Henry."

Andrei gave a pained expression and turned away. She gave him a moment as he took a long, shaky breath. "Yeah…you're right. We can keep our dreams, but we have to stay focused on the real goal. It's about more than you or me. It's about my pack and the werewolves on the grinders."

Mercy's heart broke watching him. She hadn't told him about Henry but someone must have shared the news already.

"I'm sorry," she whispered. "I'm sorry I had to do that to your friend."

He turned back to her with sad eyes. "That's how life is for us. The worst part is there's no way I could even be there for him."

She could only imagine what that had to be like, losing yourself every night and collapsing in exhaustion the next morning. Afterward, waking up the next day with only a few hours of consciousness and awareness before plunging back into another night of horror. Time had to fly by for them. Every few hours of awareness had to be cherished. Knowing that Andrei was willing to sacrifice some of that time to help her learn the notes and find a cure was an absolute testament to how good a person he was. Despite the monster he became, Andrei was a much better person than she was.

He didn't deserve to be a werewolf. There was so much more to him than that.

WITH ANDREI'S HELP, Mercy not only began to make sense of Thomas's notes, she started to understand the Liquid Lead compound she had used for years to prepare her father's darts. It wasn't a complicated mixture like she had always assumed it was growing up. It was made from chemicals that weren't hard to find. She had thought they had to be since Thomas came up with it in the basement of the pub. What surprised her was that Thomas hadn't tried to improve or modify it since its invention. All of his attempts to find a cure started from scratch, which didn't make any sense.

"Maybe Thomas was afraid to mess it up," Andrei offered. He sat in a chair in the corner of her room, his bare feet propped up on the edge of her bed. Beside him was a pile of journals and notes taken from Thomas's office.

Mercy shook her head. "More like he doesn't want to change a 'perfect' concoction. You've seen his notes. Even there he brags about the progress it's made in the city. What did he call himself? The savior of Kanta?"

She couldn't suppress a grin as she said it and Andrei laughed. His laughter was contagious. Ever since they started researching together, Mercy found herself in a better mood. She would work hard to finish her chores in the morning while Andrei slept off the exhaustion brought on by his transformation. Then she would feed the other werewolves with him, letting them out of their cages to stretch while she shared lunch with Andrei. She worked hard to see him each day, and their late after-noon study sessions together were the bright spot of her days. Mercy couldn't remember the last time she laughed so much.

Andrei closed his notebook and stood up to stretch.

"Going to get a snack?" Mercy asked as she jotted down the ingredients to Liquid Lead in her own notebook.

"It's getting late. I need to get ready for the evening."

Mercy's cheer faded. She hated that he had to be locked up every night and their time together was always so brief. It was why they fought so hard to find a cure, but it was a constant reminder of what was at stake. Every night Andrei transformed meant more strain on his body, more chances to hurt himself, and one more night where his body might not handle transforming back. Not to mention the werewolves still out in the woods dying of exposure as winter blew in.

She tried not to think of that.

The whole reason Mercy had helped Leyda bring Andrei to the mill was so Thomas could experiment on him. Only the more they examined Thomas's notes, the more they realized the sad truth: Thomas had no idea why his Liquid Lead worked or even how it worked. He was more a mechanical inventor, a businessman who dabbled in science, rather than a scientist who dabbled in business. While he took copious notes, his experimental steps and observations had no rhyme or reason. In all honesty, Thomas understood machines far better than he did werewolves, or even people. The chance of a cure from Thomas was farther off than any of them knew.

"Mercy?"

She turned to see Andrei standing in the doorway, his hand held out to her.

"Sorry, I'm coming." She closed her notebooks and hid them under her bed—a holdover of paranoia from Mitchell working at the mill—and went to join him. Together they descended the stairwell in silence and Andrei's hand was sweating in hers.

With a grunt, Andrei pulled open the giant metal door and they padded down the ramp to the laboratory. Before Andrei came to the mill, the other werewolves would be asleep by this point in the day, bedding down for the evening, but Andrei had changed all of that. Each werewolf stood in their cage watching as Mercy and Andrei hurried across the lab to Andrei's cage. The werewolf that she and her father had captured growled in the cage closest to the entrance. Mercy ignored her.

Just when Andrei stepped up into the cage, Mercy tugged on his arm and forced him to turn around. She wrapped her arms around him and hugged him tight. She didn't want to let go of him. She wanted to hold onto him and keep the harm from coming to him, but she knew she couldn't. At least not yet.

When she pulled away, Andrei was breathless and shocked as he stared at her. He swallowed hard as his eyes went glassy. "I'll see you tomorrow for lunch, okay?"

She nodded and pushed the cage door closed, forcing Andrei to step back fully into the cage. As Mercy latched it securely closed, Andrei turned around and took his clothes off, tossing them a good distance away from the cage.

He spoke with mirth in his voice. "Don't get into any trouble."

"I won't." Mercy's voice caught in her throat.

Andrei started to say something, probably to tell her not to stay. He always said that and she stayed anyway. Instead of the familiar words, Andrei screamed and clutched his head. As his back tore open and his fingers extended into claws, Mercy backed away. Blood pooled at his feet as the transformation took hold, staining the hay Mercy had put into the cage earlier. He turned and twisted from the pain.

She no longer ran away from transformations, like she had with Carter. She forced herself to stay, to witness every moment and commit it to memory. Blood streamed from Andrei's face as his jaw elongated and human teeth reconfigured into fangs. She hadn't noticed that before. She pulled a small notebook out of her pocket, the one she always kept hidden from Andrei, and added to several pages of notes.

Thomas was right about witnessing it. There were so many steps to the process, and the duration was different each time. It took longer tonight because apparently Andrei was nervous. Unknown to him, Mercy had taken notes on how he felt during each day for the past three months, and she was correlating it with his transformations.

One conclusion Mercy had come to was that the mind had some control over the process, even if it was subconscious. She thought that had to be a good sign, but she had to have more than notes and observations to do anything useful with it.

Andrei leaned down and lapped up his own blood that had pooled out from the hay. That was another observation Thomas hadn't made before. She walked up to his cage, feeling confident since Andrei's eyes were amber and not red in rage. She put a hand on the cage bars and heard the nervous sounds from the other were-wolves behind her, the ones who saw what she did every night but couldn't speak of it.

"Andrei…" she whispered as he lapped at his pooled blood. "I love you."

The werewolf looked up at her, now used to her presence after months of observations, samples, and notes. He paused to sniff her hand before returning to his meal.

"I don't know how yet, but I'm going to find a way to fix this. Just be patient with me, okay?"

The werewolf snorted, this time not lifting his head toward her.

Mercy chuckled. Even in this disturbing form, Andrei still found a way to make her laugh. "I'm just going to take a few samples if that's okay by you." She pulled out a few vials from her pocket and reached over to cut some of his fur. It would take an hour to fully get everything she needed from him, but it was easiest to get samples when he was occupied. And food always kept him occupied.

After collecting the fur, saliva, and blood samples she needed, she went into Thomas's office and closed the door behind her. She crawled onto the chair and pulled a cardboard box off the top shelf filled with rags. Moving the fabric out of the way, she unveiled the beakers, Petri dishes, and test tubes from the night before and added her non-perishable samples to the collection.

She thought she was making good progress with her own attempt at a cure. She wasn't as fast as Thomas, but she also was taking more time and caution with her experiments. Securing back her hair, she pulled down her laboratory journal to begin the night's tests. She had taken some more of the untainted werewolf blood vials from Thomas's hidden ice box in the kitchen she found one evening. It was good to have a variety of samples. There had been a promising chemical change in the previous night's experiment and she needed to explore it further to see it was meaningful or not.

Just a bit more work and Mercy might be able to help Andrei, the werewolves in the cages, the ones out in the woods, and even those still forced to work the grinders. She lit a few candles and settled in for work that would take hours tonight.

If Thomas didn't have the time or the motivation to find a cure, she would do it herself. Mercy was tired of waiting on people to help solve her problems. She would find a way to fix this herself…somehow.

IT WAS PAST MIDNIGHT by the time Mercy blew out the candles and left the laboratory. She was careful to leave the laboratory door open just a crack behind her. Yawning, she climbed the metal staircase, glad that the werewolves would sleep late tomorrow as they all did now that Andrei changed every night.

Steering away from Thomas's work put her on a better path with her experiments. In the werewolf blood samples she worked with she saw small signs of progress. The cells under a microscope had less of a reaction to silver, especially when she compared it to untreated werewolf blood samples she had used as a control. The silver response was one of the more obvious indicators of effectiveness, so it was the easiest to test. But it was merely a small sign of progress. She wanted more than silver resiliency, she wanted to take away the transformations, the loss of their minds, and ultimately their loss of humanity. True progress would take many more nights and many more experimental trials.

The metal creaked under her weight as she stopped at one of the landings. She hadn't eaten much when she and Andrei had been reading over the research earlier. It had been at least six hours since then. Better get some food real quick before bed.

When she pushed the kitchen door open, she was surprised to see an oil lantern already lit. She must have been too tired to notice the light under the door. She backed away, not wanting to draw attention to herself. Better to go to bed hungry than deal with the inevitable questions that would come about her coming to eat so late at night.

"There's no need to leave, Mercy."

It was Leyda. Mercy winced. She was right, what was the point in leaving? She knew exactly who it was already. The trouble of living with a partially transformed werewolf was that she would always know where Mercy was. There was no sneaking past her.

With a deep breath, she finished pushing through the door. Leyda sat with a plate of food at one of the metal tables. The oil lantern sat next to her and her face was uncovered.

"You're up late," she stated simply.

"So are you," Mercy replied, still standing in the doorway.

The silence stretched between them with only the distant noise of the grinders to be heard. Outside winter was bringing snow that would pile up against the grinder walls by morning. The cold seeped in through the walls of the tower. The stove fire was hot and the room was warm, but the icy stare Leyda gave her made Mercy uncertain whether or not she was welcome.

Leyda pushed her plate forward. "Want to share some food with me?"

Mercy's stomach growled as she stepped closer, trying to get a good look at the plate. "What is it?"

"Roasted chicken. A rarity around these parts. Let me get you some." Leyda reached behind her, pulled a plate and a fork down, and dropped several pieces of meat onto Mercy's plate.

Mercy got a glass of water and sat down across from her, taking the plate with a polite nod. "Thank you."

Leyda spoke not a word, her expression as she watched Mercy was unreadable. Finally Mercy couldn't take the scrutiny any longer.

"Did you want to talk about something?"

"Yes," Leyda said, but then didn't say anything more.

Mercy sipped at her cup of water, feeling her annoyance growing. "And?" she prodded.

Leyda sighed and turned to look at the wall. "I'm sorry I didn't mention you were outside. To Thomas, I mean. You know. After I brought Andrei in that first night. I'm sorry about that."

Mercy nearly choked on her water. "Leyda, that was months ago. I moved past that a while ago. It's fine."

"You could have died. You were attacked by a werewolf. People were killed, and you could have been one of them. It isn't fine."

"I don't hold any hard feelings about it. It really isn't a big deal. I wish you would move on."

"No, it's clearly affected you, changed you. You're up late every night. I hear you climbing the staircase in the wee hours of the morning. What are you doing all night long?"

Mercy suddenly wished she hadn't stopped by the kitchen at all. Had Leyda been spying on her? That made her uncomfortable. "I'm working."

"What cleaning is there to do at midnight, child? None. And you spend all your days in your room with Andrei. Don't think I haven't noticed that. It's not a good idea. It won't end well."

"Why, because he's a werewolf?"

"No, because he's an experiment."

Mercy slammed her fork down. "Why are you always like this?"

"Like what?" Leyda sat back in her chair.

"You talk about this gloom and doom all the time! Why do you say these things?"

"Because I want to help you."

"You don't even know me."

Leyda crossed her arms and cocked her head to the side. "Of course I know you. We live here together, don't we? I saved your life and you work alongside me. I know you well enough."

"Okay, then how old am I?"

She smiled, revealing her sharp teeth. "That's easy. Thirteen."

"No, I'm fourteen. My birthday was last week. January fourth."

Leyda grunted in frustration. "What is the point? Thirteen, fourteen, it's all the same."

"My point is I'm working all the time, and I'd appreciate it if you didn't stalk me." Mercy got to her feet, picked up her plate and fork, and dropped them into the sink. "The next time you want to apologize about something, please don't wait three months to do it. If you know me so well, then you should know it's too late to apologize for it now. I wanted to forget about it."

"There's no running from your past, child."

Mercy turned for the door and gripped the doorknob in one hand when Leyda spoke in a soft tone.

"I'm sorry I missed your birthday, Mercy."

She winced, regretting losing her temper but also hoping that she had shaken Leyda off her trail for a while. "And I'm sorry Andrei hurt you when you brought him in." She glanced over her shoulder and

Leyda gave her a slow nod. Mercy took a deep breath and headed out.

She hoped that whatever friction had grown between her and Leyda was finally settled. Regardless, she would have to be more careful when she headed to bed late at night, and more careful about her research and notes. She couldn't let Leyda know what she was working on. If she didn't approve of Andrei spending so much time with her, she certainly wouldn't approve of Mercy's work. She still saw her as a werewolf hunter, nothing more.

Leyda simply wouldn't understand.

9

———————

CONFESSION

"IT DOESN'T MATTER how far you throw them, you always find a way to get holes in your clothes," Mercy laughed over a hot mug of soup.

Andrei smiled, the steam from his mug dancing in front of his face. "I don't know how I do it either, to be honest. I promise it's not on purpose." His cage door was open and he sat with his feet on the stone floor. He wore a coat over his linen shirt and had a blanket over his shoulders, but it only did so much. The room was colder than normal from the snowstorm that had blown in overnight, but that wasn't the only reason he was shivering. Unless he had a blanket or a hot drink, he usually couldn't stop shivering. Worse yet, he was getting weaker every week, and the onset of winter hadn't helped. The exhaustion was the worst right after his transformation, which was why Mercy was keen to bring something hot to warm him up each afternoon. Today he had slept so late she had been afraid he wouldn't wake at all.

He laughed and Mercy tried not to see the strain and exhaustion in his eyes. His brown skin held a yellowish tone, his freckles had faded, his eyes were more sunken, and he definitely moved slower than he used to. Just walking from room to room took a toll on him.

As much as Mercy tried to keep her analytical mind separated from her friendly face during the day, it was getting harder to do as she watched the person she considered her only real friend, the person she confessed her love to every night, waste away in front of her eyes. She found herself wondering what the average life expectancy was for werewolves. Thomas had books that listed it for humans but not werewolves. Apparently nobody had cared to study them. It made her angry.

"Mercy?"

She turned to look at him. "What?" she asked, realizing too late that he was talking and she hadn't noticed.

He gave her that cute grin again, the one that always melted her heart. "I lost you again, didn't I?"

"Sorry." She put her mug down.

"You want to share what's going on in your head?"

Her cheeks warmed. "Not really."

"Hmm." Andrei slurped down the rest of his soup. Clearly being an assistant at an apothecary didn't require manners. Her father would have snapped at her for eating soup that loudly.

Putting his mug aside, he crossed his arms over his knees. "Is it Thomas or Leyda that's troubling you?"

She blinked at him. "What? Oh, no, they're fine."

"Okay, so did you have to go into town again?"

She shook her head and gave an awkward laugh. "Why would I need to go into town?"

He stared at her, his warm caramel eyes bore into hers. Mercy tried her best but couldn't help fidgeting under his intense stare.

"Then what is it, Mercy? You've been acting cagey for weeks and you keep zoning out when I'm finally able to see you. Now I know I'm not around for most of the day, but I was a guard for a bunch of paranoid were-wolves for a while, so I know when you're hiding something."

Mercy broke out in a sweat. She had worked so hard to hide her work from Leyda that she had forgotten how perceptive Andrei could be.

"Now I know I'm not always the quickest about things—"

"Andrei…"

"But you would still be struggling to read those journals of notes without my help, so I think I deserve a little bit of trust here, don't you?"

Mercy shook her head. "Pulling out the guilt card, huh?"

He arched his eyebrows. "I can carry on if you really want me to."

Mercy held up a hand. "No, there's no need to get that serious."

Andrei arched his eyebrows and gestured to her, waiting patiently. She took a deep breath, already knowing he wouldn't like the details of all she had to say. So much happened in the hours when he transformed and slept. Her life had turned into a literal night and day difference.

"You know we've been doing research together."

He nodded.

"After hours, I've been doing more…hands on research on my own."

He narrowed his eyes and leaned forward. "Hands on…what do you mean?"

She pursed her lips and gave a rosy account of her small experimental vials she kept hidden away in Thomas's office.

"Just a minute." He leaned back, putting his hands behind him onto the metal floor of the cage. "You barely knew what chemicals were a few months ago. Now you say you're combining them together?" He glanced over to the door along the far wall. "And you're doing all that in Thomas's office?"

"It's been six months to be exact, not just a few. And you're right, I didn't know what I was doing at first, but I've learned so much! Every time you transform—"

"So you *have* been watching me each night. After I clearly asked you not to." He averted his eyes. "I always hoped you ran off, but I guess not."

Mercy felt her heart skip a beat. "How can you expect me to help you if I don't know how it works?" Her voice wavered as she spoke. She hadn't realized how strongly she felt about it until she heard it in her own voice.

Andrei was silent for a long moment before taking a deep sigh. "It feels like a violation of my privacy. I didn't want you to see me like that. That's why I asked you not to watch me."

She crouched down in front of him and wrapped her hands around his. "I still like you regardless of all that."

He glanced up to her, his brow scrunched up with worry.

"I know you don't like it. To be honest it's been hard to watch sometimes."

He swallowed. "I hate that you've seen that monster come out of me. I was hoping…I didn't want you to have to see me like that. It's not me, it's just a creature that lives in me. I may be a werewolf, but that werewolf isn't me."

She squeezed his hands, trying to calm him down. "I'm trying to help you. I have to observe to learn. How else can I find a cure for it if I don't see it for myself? Do you know how little research I can find in books? Thomas has enough money to buy any scientific journal out there, but there is hardly anything published on werewolves. Nobody does research on them. I'm working blind for the most part."

When she put a hand to his cheek, his skin felt chill under her touch. She wiped a tear from his cheek with her thumb. "You've seen Thomas's notes and how inconsistent his observations are. And we're running out of time. We have to find a cure before——" Her throat clamped up before she could continue.

"Before what?" he whispered, searching her face for an answer. Mercy pulled away from him.

"Before this curse kills you," she hissed. Her voice betrayed the maelstrom of emotions roiling inside her.

Andrei blinked and his mouth dropped open. She could almost see him putting the pieces together in his head, but she elaborated anyway even though her voice wavered and her throat felt tight.

"Every time you change, you get weaker. Every night I worry it will be the last time I see you. You have fueled me to do this. I know it isn't right and I knew you would be mad at me. You probably feel betrayed right now, but even if you hate me for the rest of your life, it's worth it knowing you're alive."

Andrei stared at her for a long moment and his eyes were welling with tears again. "*If* you can find a cure. You don't know that there is one yet. You're only one person, Mercy, and you're a novice at this."

She felt a flare of anger at his words but pushed down the feeling. He didn't know how much time she spent every night poring over the notes, making her own, doing trials, experimenting with chemicals she had never used before.

Mercy turned away from him to collect herself. She had taken blood samples, fur samples, and even saliva samples from him when he had been in his wolf form. She considered asking him multiple times for his permission, but he had volunteered to be an experiment. She had used that as an excuse. Now here he was asking her to air all her dark secrets. If he was angry about her just witnessing his change in the laboratory, what would he think if he knew the full extent of her work? Would the person she whispered to in the dead of night forgive her?

Andrei believed in morals much more than she did. To her they were road blocks that needed to be avoided. To him they were infallible guidelines. He valued respect and privacy while she valued innovation despite the sacrifice. He clearly knew what was right and wrong. Mercy wasn't always sure she had a good grasp on that.

If she was completely honest with herself, her values were more in line with people like Thomas and Leyda. Did that make her heartless? She didn't think so. She just refused to be naïve like she used to be. She refused to ever be a victim again, even if it meant bending the rules and hurting someone's feelings. Even if it meant being cruel.

"Mercy, what exactly have you been up to while I've been out each night? I need to know everything."

She sighed and managed a small shrug. "I have…something."

He put a hand on her arm. His grip was gentle but she heard the anxiety in his voice. "Please, talk to me. I've been there for the research. What exactly have you found?"

She slid her hand over his, feeling the roughness of his skin. There was something comforting about Andrei, something that made her barriers and shields crumble. He grounded her when she sometimes feared her mind could float away from her.

"Promise me you won't be mad," she said, studying his face.

A mixture of emotions passed over him, from shock

to outrage to a brief moment of anger. Finally it settled into resolution and he clenched his jaw before nodding. "I promise. I won't be mad. Just please tell me what you found."

"Okay," she bit her lip. "I've been doing more than just observing your change each night. I've been documenting you, how you feel every day, what hurts, how long you sleep. I monitor your activity, your food and water intake, your mental activity. I study your moods, your thoughts…I track everything about you."

He dragged a hand through his hair. "Mercy, you could have asked me first. I don't mind being a test subject, that's why I came here after all. But I'd prefer it if you got my approval first. I thought we were friends."

She picked up his hand and put it on her shoulder, leaning her head against his forearm. She breathed in his scent. He needed a bath but she didn't care. She wanted to be close to him. She wanted to remind herself of him in case he never wanted to speak to her again. Just in case he left her. Cause he always could, and to be honest he had every right to considering how much she hadn't told him. "You've only been present for half of the research."

Andrei shifted, but didn't say anything so she continued.

"Thomas has samples of werewolf blood from each one he's taken into the mill. They go back years. Some of them are probably long dead from working the grinders."

Andrei shifted again, but she had started this and she had to finish it.

"I've been using them to test the attempts I've made for a cure. I tried different combinations of things, starting with Thomas's early mixture and then working out from there. His observations were scattered. He occasionally noted things that were helpful. Sometimes I even take samples from you after you've transformed." Hearing a sharp inhale, Mercy glanced up to see Andrei's shocked face, "I've taken blood, saliva, hair, urine… sometimes even tissue."

He pulled his hand away and Mercy felt a pang in her chest at his fury. "That's dangerous! I'm not mindless like those werewolves in the grinders, I could kill you in an instant."

"I know, but you're used to me now. You like me."

He shook his head. "I'm a wild animal. I don't like anything or anyone. I could kill you. I can't believe you would risk yourself like that!"

She held her hands up. "But I had to! I had to make sure it would work on you, and it did."

He shook his head. "Hang on a moment," his voice trembled. "Are you telling me you found a cure?"

"No, I found something. If it was a definite cure, don't you think I would have given it to you by now?"

He laughed and Mercy found herself smiling along with him. That's what she would miss the most if something happened to him, or if he refused to be near her again. That was what she loved the most. His laugh made her feel like she could do anything. He pulled her close and kissed her and she kissed him back. Her mind reeled, not sure if he was still angry or not. Gently he pulled away and pushed a hand into her hair.

"You're a genius, Mercy."

She shook her head in disbelief. "You don't even know what I made yet."

"Doesn't matter. You've done in months what nobody else has tried to do for years."

"If they did try, they weren't successful," she added. "And I don't know if what I've made is successful or not."

"What do you mean?"

She frowned. She thought about explaining the chemical combinations that she had sorted out and given up on, the dead ends, the failed attempts, but that was too complicated. So she tried to keep it simple. Every afternoon they had limited time together.

"I first saw reactions in the blood with low levels of certain chemicals, so I tried stronger versions, chemical combinations, mixing and matching without making anything too dangerous until the smallest amount showed the most change. Then I moved from blood to other areas, such as fur, urine, saliva, and finally tissue. Obviously, you were the only werewolf not treated with Liquid Lead who I could get those kinds of samples from, so the results aren't complete. And I'm only seeing the reactions on tiny samples, not a full person."

Andrei blinked, clearly overwhelmed.

"Maybe it'll be easier if I just show you."

She got to her feet and held out her hand to help Andrei up. Sometimes just getting to his feet was a challenge these days. In Thomas's office, she lit a few candles so they could have sufficient light. She pulled over the large armchair to retrieve her box on the top shelf of a rickety bookshelf.

"Be careful," Andrei urged and she snickered. He still cared for her, despite all of her confessions. She calmed her heart as she reached up to the top shelf.

He leaned against the wall, barely able to walk on his own without help, yet here he was worried about her climbing on top of furniture. He was adorable. She had done this every night for months.

"Trust me okay? I do this all the time."

She pulled her box down and removed the rags on top that she used to keep everything hidden and secure.

Andrei looked around the room, and Mercy realized he hadn't been into Thomas's office very often. They fetched notebooks, research journals, or other documentation, but they never stayed long. She had gotten used to the jumbled mess of overflowing bookshelves, stacks of papers, and the smell of dust and old ink. Thomas had clearly forgotten about much of the supplies he had hidden in the back corners. Dusty glass beakers, toppled bunsen burners, and stoppered chemical jars were all labeled in his messy handwriting. Mercy had spent hours finding everything, organizing it for herself, and noting everything down in her notebooks. But she supposed to anyone else it was still very much a mess.

"Does Thomas know you come down here and work on this?"

Mercy pulled the last bundle of rags out of the box. "If he knew I did this, do you think he would let me? What Thomas doesn't know can't hurt him. Besides, I'd rather ask for forgiveness once I have something to show for my work than beforehand."

"Couldn't some of these chemicals be toxic?"

"I don't use them if they are. I'm trying to heal werewolves not kill them. If they're toxic to me, it'll be toxic to them too."

Andrei settled down in Thomas's chair, clearly relieved to be off his feet. "He did ask you to be a researcher, so maybe it wouldn't be a problem."

She shook her head, once again admiring his eternal optimism about people. "He wants me to be a researcher so I can give him ideas of what to make, not do it myself. He's barely down here at all anymore, but I guess that's my fault. Ever since I told him he needed to update the grinders so he can gain the trust of werewolves, that's all he focuses on now. He must have someplace else where he works on mechanical arms because I couldn't find any wires or tubing here at all. I looked in all the boxes, but it's mostly old books, journals, and chemistry supplies. That's all I needed though, so I didn't worry about finding his other workshop."

Andrei grinned and his eyes sparkled in the candle-light. "You've really ransacked this place, haven't you? I didn't realize you were so resourceful."

She rolled her eyes. "Okay, watch this. Here we have a few drops of werewolf blood in this vial. It's only been here a few hours so it should still be good from last night. This will be our control. Let me add a few drops to this empty vial too."

She dripped a few drops into each vial as Andrei leaned in close to watch.

"Is that my blood?" he asked.

She rolled her eyes, "No, it's not your blood. Calm down and focus."

He cleared his throat. "Okay, sorry."

She set the vial down and picked up another one with a clear fluid inside. "Now I'm going to add a few drops of the compound I made."

"Compound, huh? Don't you sound like a professional?"

She nudged him with her foot even though she couldn't suppress a smirk. "Okay, this next part may be upsetting, but try not to get nervous. This is how I have to test it to make sure it works."

She opened a black velvet drawstring satchel and pulled out a long chunk of solid silver. Andrei gasped. His eyes went wide and his grin turned into a grimace. He recoiled, curling back and flattening himself against the seat cushion.

"What's that for?" His voice was a ghost of its former self and Mercy gave him a stern gaze.

"Do you want me to stop the demonstration? I can if this is too much for you."

He stared at the chunk of silver, breathing hard, eyes wide, and clutching at his elbows. It was if she had pulled out a gun and aimed it at him.

"No, it's fine…" His voice was hollow but his eyes didn't leave the silver. "I haven't been near a piece of silver like that before. It really freaks me out. But how weird is that? It's just a rock, right? It shouldn't get to me like this." He gave a nervous laugh.

She hid the piece of silver behind her. "I feel like you're talking to the silver more than me."

He blinked and turned to face her, shaking himself. "Sorry. Okay, I'm ready this time. Please show me. I want to know what happens."

Mercy studied him. He was shaking, but his eyes were clear. Despite clearly being overwhelmed, she understood his need to know the truth. She admired him for it, knowing how hard it was to overcome an innate fear. She decided it was best to be quick. She pulled out the silver again and held it over the control sample. "This is a normal werewolf reaction to silver."

She lowered the silver into the vial. As soon as it touched the liquid, the blood changed color from dark red to a smoky reddish-black. A hissing sound emerged. Soon the drops of blood had turned black as pitch. She removed the silver and the blood wanted to stick to it like tar. Andrei was breathing rapidly, but she ignored him. He wanted to see this, so she was going to show him. If he wanted to know, he had to deal with the horrors. It was the price of knowledge.

Mercy wiped off the stone with a clean cloth. "So that's what normally happens when a werewolf is hit with silver."

"Instant death," Andrei muttered. "It's horrible."

"I know. I was surprised too." The first time she introduced the silver, she had expected she would need to pull out Thomas's microscope to see any changes, but she didn't. It was unsettling. She tried hard not to think of Henry. Or about all the female werewolves her father had put down when he captured werewolves in the woods instead of males.

"So this next vial has a few drops of my compound in it." She lowered the silver into the vial while Andrei watched intently. Inside the blood stayed red and didn't seem affected at all.

"You did it," Andrei breathed. "You found a cure."

Mercy removed the silver and wiped it down on a cloth. Then placed it back into the black velvet bag and put it away. "Like I said before, I've found something. Is it a cure? I have no idea. I have to test it first."

Andrei shook his head. "You're too modest. It's a cure, it has to be."

"We don't know that for certain. All we know is that the blood doesn't seem to be bothered by silver." She held up a hand to him, "And no, you're not going to volunteer to try it first."

"Why not? Mercy, I volunteered to be a test subject."

"You did. And you balked at me having to observe you every night. I don't want to hurt you with this." She pulled out the vial with her compound and put a stopper into it. Then she grabbed a few of her homemade darts and dropped them into her pocket.

Andrei watched her carefully. "So clearly you plan on testing it on someone. If you won't test it on me, who will you test it on?"

Mercy pushed him out of the chair so she could put her box, now padded with rags, back on the top shelf. "You're not going to like it."

He crossed his arms, cocking an eyebrow. "Try me."

She dropped back down to the floor. "Thomas is

working on updating the grinders. That means there will be a lot of werewolves without a purpose. Instead of letting them be destroyed, I thought I'd see what my drug does to them first. I was going to go tonight, but it might be easier during the day. You could help that way, just in case."

"Do you even hear yourself? Those poor bastards don't have long, they barely have minds anymore after being forced to not sleep for days. And instead of showing them compassion and putting them out of their misery, *now* you want to give them a potential cure? They don't even have the ability to consent to any of this. I do! Just give it to me and let's see what it does."

"No." She went for the door but Andrei stepped in front of her. "What are you doing?"

"Why can't you just let me try it?"

"I refuse." She tried to side step him, but he followed her movements.

"Why?" he demanded. "You're willing to use it on nameless werewolves who have been tortured on those grinders, why won't you give it to me too?"

"Because…" She hesitated; if she told him, everything might change. But his gaze never wavered. "Because I love you."

Andrei's eyes went wide and the small office went silent as they stared at each other. Mercy's heart pounded in her chest. She had never expected to say it aloud, but now it was done. There was no taking it back.

"Mercy, I—" He went silent, unable to say more.

She fished the clear vial out of her pocket and held it up to him. "This could kill you. I don't know how much I need for each werewolf. I don't know what the reaction will be. I don't know anything more about it, all I know is that it prevents an instant silver death. Even if it turns you back into a human, you could still lose your mind like the ones on the grinders." Her voice wavered. "I can't let that happen to you. I don't care if you volunteered. I don't care if you want to die, or whatever else compels you to do this. I care, and I don't want to hurt you."

"Mercy…I'm sorry. I should have known."

He put his arms around her, and she let him fold her against him. He hugged her tight and she leaned against his warmth, his security.

"Please don't make me hurt you," she hissed against his chest, trying hard not to cry. "Please don't make me do something I'll regret."

He held her tight and she closed her eyes against him, breathing in his scent.

"If this hurt you, I would never forgive myself."

"Shh, it's okay." He kissed the top of her head, "I'm sorry I'm so dense sometimes."

Mercy grinned and shook her head, feeling his chest through the layers of shirts he wore, reveling in his warmth and his presence. She knew the final secret she had to tell him. "Every night I told you that I loved you. It seems so silly saying that aloud, but it felt safer then. You were a werewolf so you couldn't understand me." She pulled back to see him smiling.

He put a hand against her cheek and she put her hand on his, linking their fingers together.

"Thank you for looking out for me. Sometimes I

forget that people care about me. Sometimes I forget to care about myself too, I guess."

She dragged his hand over to kiss his fingers. "You keep me grounded. Without you, I'm afraid I would lose myself."

"That's not going to happen. I'm not going anywhere, in fact I—" Andrei paused and cocked his head to the side.

"What is it?" She asked.

"One of the grinders. I think it stopped."

10

———————

MONSTROUS

AS THEY WALKED UP the spiral staircase and toward the grinders, it became more obvious one of the giant machines was off. After months of listening to them churn and belch steam into the sky, Mercy knew the sound well, and the pitch was definitely off. She hadn't heard it down in Thomas's laboratory, but as they climbed the tower, it was obvious.

She pulled her fur coat closer around herself when they stepped outside. The snowstorm overnight left the sky a cloudy steel gray, and she could see her breath in the air. She glanced back over her shoulder at Andrei. "Are you going to be okay coming out here?"

He nodded, buttoning up his coat. "Lead the way."

They passed over the catwalks for the third and second grinders before reaching the oldest one, the first grinder she had seen when she first came to the mill. As they entered the giant cylindrical chamber, the lack of noise compared to the other grinders was disconcerting.

"I didn't realize how loud they normally are,"

Andrei said. They made their way to the ladder that would take them down to the base of the grinder.

Snowfall had blanketed the normally muddy base, leaving behind a layer of snow that hadn't melted. The first thing Mercy noticed was the werewolves were gone. The neck restraints used to keep them pinned to the grinder were missing too. Even when she helped to clean the sides of the pit, the neck restraints normally remained.

The grinder itself was new. A plethora of new, shiny gears and metal tubing glinted in the afternoon light. It looked completely different from the old grinder that used to be suspended over the pit. The machine was currently off, but based on seeing Thomas's work before, Mercy could guess how quickly it would move once it was turned on. Down below she spotted Thomas's familiar red hair at the base. He was walking through the snow surveying his work. He was alone.

She turned to Andrei. "Can you climb down?"

He was shivering again and blinked at her. She gestured to the service ladder. It was a long way down and the unspoken question was whether or not he could climb back up again after.

"I might be a little slower than you, but I'll manage."

"If it's too difficult, don't be afraid to say so. I don't want you getting hurt."

"Don't worry. I'll be the first to complain."

Mercy headed down first. She wasn't as fast a climber as Thomas or Leyda but she was quicker than when she first started working at the mill. Her feet crunched down on snow as she hit the ground and she turned to see Thomas approaching her with a wide grin and open arms.

"Isn't it beautiful? It runs completely werewolf free as you can clearly see. Steam powered, of course. It'll take a while to get the fuel hot enough to where we can flip a switch, but isn't it gorgeous?"

"It's impressive," she admitted. Looking up from the base of the grinders always made her anxious simply because so much metal hung over her head. It didn't help that the new grinder was bigger than the old one.

Thomas put an arm around her shoulders and called up to Andrei. "Take your time. There's no rush! We're certainly not going anywhere."

Mercy felt the vial and darts in her pockets knock against her leg. She had been so distracted by the grinder itself that she almost forgot why she came down. The question was on her lips before she realized it. "But what did you do with the werewolves?"

Thomas's smile faltered just a little and his lazy eye drifted to the side. "Oh, Mercy, this was the first grinder. These werewolves have been here for weeks, maybe over a month now. They were some of the most docile, sure, but they were also the closest to death's door, I'm afraid."

Andrei's boots crunched down on the snow behind them. She turned to see him rub his hands together as he came over to join them. "You didn't have them destroyed, did you, Mr. Farrell?" His voice was accusatory.

Slowly Thomas retracted his arm from Mercy's shoulders and he gave a nervous laugh. "Goodness,

Andrei, no. There's no need to make me sound like a monster. Surely Mercy told you how I plan to make each grinder be completely werewolf free eventually."

Mercy caught Andrei's eye and saw him give a brief nod. It wasn't Thomas's plan to begin with. Mercy had to convince him to take this path. Yet how quickly the tune changed to Thomas being the kind and benevolent mill owner who saw the error of his ways. If she told him about the experimental compound she carried with her, she knew it would be treated the exact same way.

"I don't mean to offend, Mr. Farrell." Andrei put his hands into his pockets, looking casual and comfortable out here when Mercy knew he was anything but that. "I'm just curious about what happened to them considering it was your idea to shackle them down here in this pit to begin with."

Mercy could kiss him.

"Please, just Thomas. My father was Mr. Farrell." Thomas gave a nervous laugh, clearly hoping to change the subject. But Andrei wasn't some random werewolf hunter off the street easy to impress. He was precisely the person who, with a little less luck, could have met the same fate as any of the werewolves on the grinders.

It was difficult for Mercy not to clearly choose a side, not to second Andrei's words. Instead she forced herself to remain quiet and not tip her hand. Thomas needed to see her as an ally in some form, so she could continue working and living under his roof. She still needed access to his supplies and his office so she couldn't risk his trust.

With a hefty sigh, Thomas turned to the inactive

grinder. The previous machine must have witnessed dozens if not hundreds of werewolves over the years. Mercy tried not to think of that. Hands on his hips, Thomas spoke with more clarity than she had heard from him in a long time.

"Believe it or not, I'm not in the business of murder here. I've never been keen on it. One of the reasons I made Liquid Lead to begin with was because I was tired of being surrounded by death every night."

He walked around the grinder and Andrei and Mercy followed in silence, their feet crunching in the snow.

"I know how ridiculous that sounds." He laughed. "Those were strange times. We had our lives threatened every night. It was either kill or be killed back in those days." He gestured to them. "Yes, I made it to save us, I don't deny that. But I also made it to keep the ground from being a bloody swamp day in and day out. Even the rain couldn't get rid of it. And the stench!" He wrapped his arms around his stomach. "I don't think I'll ever be able to forget it. Werewolf blood is quite pungent."

Mercy nodded. "Do you think that's why you've been struggling to make advances on a cure?" she asked carefully.

Thomas glanced at her with wide, fearful eyes as though she just called him a fraud. "You are…what exactly are you implying, Mercy?"

"Andrei has been helping me on the research. I was going to work with you more closely, but—"

"But I'm never down there in the lab anymore, am

I?" Thomas took a deep breath, as though saying the words would expel them from his system.

"You always seemed so excited about each transformation, each step of research, I thought you always relished it."

Thomas shook a finger at her. "I relished the thought of a cure and of being praised for it as I was for Liquid Lead, my dear. I don't believe anyone can enjoy a werewolf transformation."

"I agree with that," Andrei said with a heavy sigh.

It was in that moment that Mercy realized she had surpassed Thomas's research months ago. Even with her subpar reading skills at the start and her minimal experience with chemicals, she had still surpassed him in sheer determination through observation, notes, and a willingness to experiment. Although Thomas had made an incredible breakthrough with Liquid Lead, he was having a hard time moving beyond it. He was struggling to discover more.

Mercy wasn't sure if Thomas set too high of a goal for himself or if the environment and terror of the constant werewolf attacks propelled him to make Liquid Lead to begin with. Regardless, he had tried for years to find a cure and always hit walls. She had read his growing frustration and self-doubt in his notes, but it was still alarming to hear it in person. Thomas seemed like such a confident person when she first met him, but now she better understood his business persona, the face he wore to Kanta, and his eagerness to hand the research off to someone else. It was rare that he spoke of his true feelings.

"So if you aren't destroying them," Andrei asked, "then what are you doing with them?"

Thomas dragged a hand through his hair and eyed them with wariness. "I can't kill them, not knowing what I do now. I had them moved to cages in the back there." He pointed to a shadowy corner of the pit beneath the catwalk. The sunlight reflected off the snow drifts and made it hard to see them. Mercy had to shield her eyes to see the yellow eyes peering out.

The mushy ground squished beneath her shoes as Mercy approached them. The snow had been worn down as the werewolves were gathered, but the cages reminded her of shipping containers, all shoved against the wall. Andrei followed her over as Thomas continued.

"Since I can't destroy them, I'm keeping them out of view from any visitors. I can't have others know what I'm doing. Not yet at least. I can keep them comfortable until they're fully healed, but after that, I don't know what to do."

Andrei seemed clearly shaken to see so many of his kind armless and shoved into a corner like so much storage. Still he tried to keep the conversation going and Mercy wasn't sure if he was curious or if his nerves made his mouth run.

"It seems wrong to release them into the woods. Especially since they can't change back from this."

"Oh no, I can't do that! They could kill people here in town or attack travelers. They could even go after your werewolf pack during the day. It would be far too dangerous."

Mercy stepped closer to the cages. She counted twelve of them. Even if visitors did notice the crates down here, it would be hard to tell what was inside of them. Twelve pairs of dim, golden eyes stared at her, all of them without arms. Some leaned against the cage walls, others were flopped on the ground. None of them growled at her but she knew that didn't mean they were safe to approach.

The vial of compound felt heavy in her pocket and her hands itched to pull it out, along with the darts. As passive as they were right now fresh off the grinder, they probably wouldn't resist very much. Thomas might even let her move one of them to the laboratory for observation. She reached down into her pocket and took hold of the vial.

"Mr. Farrell! What do you want us to do with the old parts?" A voice called down from the catwalk.

Mercy's heart skipped a beat. She hadn't considered there would be workers around here still. For some reason she assumed Thomas had been working alone on upgrading the grinders, which was ridiculous. He would certainly have needed a whole team to get the equipment changed out, and to get the werewolves in their cages. Thomas couldn't do everything on his own.

Grabbing Andrei's arm, she dragged him to the wall a few feet down from the werewolf cages. Twelve pairs of golden eyes watched them with intense interest. She wondered when they were last fed.

"Mr. Farrell, are you down there, sir?"

Thomas didn't respond until they were both pressed up against the wall, then he stepped out into the daylight with confidence. "Sorry, Murphy, I didn't hear you! I'll be up in a minute."

"With all respect, sir, we don't have all day. Some of us need to get home before nightfall."

"Yes, yes, I'm coming." Thomas climbed up the ladder.

As he climbed, Mercy tried not to notice how nice it felt to have Andrei's arm wrapped around hers. She couldn't deny how much she enjoyed slinking around in the shadows with him either. Squeezing his arm, she wondered if he enjoyed this as much as she did, but he didn't turn to her. Perhaps he didn't.

Only when they heard Thomas talking with the worker up on the catwalk did Andrei turn to her.

"Why do we have to hide from him?" he whispered as he kept glancing up to the catwalk above.

"A young woman working at the mill? Everyone would start asking questions. I don't want to attract the attention of any more hunters or traffickers. That was bad enough last time."

"I remember you mentioned that Carter and Mitchell tried to kill you, but I don't really get why."

"Because I'm a young woman who prevented them from selling me off."

His eyes went wide. "Like as a servant?"

She shook her head. "Something like that. I really don't want to talk about it."

He gave a slow nod and thankfully dropped the topic. Even though it had been months since the whole ordeal, Mercy still got tense just talking about it all. Even though she knew it was a cruel thought, she hoped

Carter had already died on one of the grinders. She would have to ask Leyda later. She would understand. Andrei wouldn't. He might even think her terrible for asking.

Thomas led Murphy down the catwalk toward the front reception room for the mill. Mercy stepped forward and watched to make sure they left through the door, then breathed a sigh of relief.

"Okay, we should be good now."

"Good." Andrei laughed. "If it took too much longer you were going to have to find a spare werewolf cage for me down here."

She gave him a bittersweet smile. Honestly she wasn't sure how he could joke about his condition when Mercy couldn't even think about Mitchell and Carter without grinding her teeth.

He stepped toward the ladder. "I guess we need to get out of here before they come back."

Mercy shook her head. "No, not yet…" She pulled out the vial and a dart from her pockets. "I've got to figure out which one of these guys I'll test this on first."

Andrei clamped a hand on her wrist, tight enough to hurt.

"Ow, Andrei, let go!" He loosened his grip immediately and she wrenched her arm free. She rubbed at her wrist, grateful that she hadn't dropped the vial. "What's wrong with you?" Already hot tempered from talking about Mitchell and Carter, she really didn't need Andrei adding to it.

"Sorry, I just…" He trailed off and stuffed his hands back into his pockets. "I can't let you use that on them."

Mercy sighed. "Really? We're back on this again? I know they can't give their consent to being experimented on, but they're not going to live much longer as it is. It's harsh, but doesn't that make the most sense?"

Andrei shook his head slowly and bit his lip.

"Okay, then what's the problem? Why stop me from testing a possible cure?"

He looked to the werewolves, then up to the catwalk, and his eyes misted over. "No, you're not thinking this through." He paused, still gnawing on his lip, and it took all the restraint Mercy had to not go over and jab a dart into one of the werewolves.

"What if it works?" he asked at last.

Mercy stared at him in disbelief. "If it works, we celebrate!"

"No, listen." He squeezed his eyes shut as if to force the words out. "What if this works on one of these werewolves and it changes them back? They aren't like me, Mercy, they've been strapped to a grinder for weeks, or months, or however long it takes a werewolf to die when they're being worked to the bone day in and day out. They may not have their minds anymore, Mercy. They may not be able to speak or control their bodily functions. Just look at them, they can barely stand!"

She looked over them, past their dim amber eyes and unnerving stares. The few who were flopped on the ground hadn't even tried to stand when she and Andrei stood merely feet away from their cages. In werewolf form they had the advantage of physical prowess far above what humans could achieve. What would happen to them if she took away that physical advantage and dropped them into their weaker human forms?

"I mean, they don't even have arms. Can you imagine coming back to your senses and realizing you had lost a pair of limbs along the way? That's horrible." He dragged a hand across his face. "I panicked when I lost an eye and it took weeks to grow back. It was painful. I know you're trying to help and your heart is in the right place, but I don't think you're thinking this through all the way, Mercy. Don't be so eager to try your newest potential cure so much that you ruin their lives. If it does work, we can help all of these guys to heal up and get well before we give it to them. At least then we can prevent putting them through mental anguish and even more physical pain."

Mercy put the vial and dart back into her pocket. "You're right. I don't know what I was thinking. I guess I'm just desperate to find another test subject so you don't feel like you have to do it."

As she said it, shame filled her as she realized what she was about to do. She looked at the werewolves with Andrei's perspective and instead of seeing ideal test subjects caged and docile, easy to stick with a dart, she saw them as who they really were: unfortunate humans who had been poisoned, brutalized, and tortured. They had been used as free manual labor, had their arms ripped off, and had their minds taken from them.

They didn't deserve to be experimented on further. They deserved to be allowed to heal, to recover from the brutality they had endured. If her concoction worked without any additional side effects, only then should she use it on them.

Andrei put an arm around her and squeezed.

"I'm sorry. You're absolutely right. I can't believe I was about to do something so…monstrous."

"Don't be like that. You just wanted to help." He gently turned her away from the caged werewolves and back toward the ladder. "Come on, let's go to the kitchen and see if there's anything good to eat."

Mercy couldn't help but chuckle. "We just had lunch a little while ago."

"Hey, I had a big appetite before I got bitten. Now I'm an endless pit."

Mercy went to the ladder and started climbing up. Her gaze still drifted toward the door that led to the reception room for the mill. Once she had climbed halfway up and the familiar burn settled into her arms, she looked down to Andrei and frowned. He was only ten or fifteen rungs up, way behind her, but he was moving at a slow pace. If they weren't so close to that door, she would have called down to make sure he was okay.

She remembered how weak he looked in the laboratory earlier, barely able to get to his feet. Now he was having to climb up a ladder he really was in no shape to climb. She should have gone behind him to check on him, but she had been lost in her own thoughts and problems.

Reaching the top, she waited for him even though it was a huge risk to be standing right by the doors. She fancied she could hear Thomas and Murphy talking on the other side, and she hoped they wouldn't open the door on her. Andrei climbed a good ten rungs, then had to loop his arm through and hang for a while to get his breath before he could climb another few rungs. The cold wind and icy metal rungs probably didn't help. He was really doing well considering the state he was in, and she felt bad dragging him out here when he was clearly not well enough for it.

Finally when he reached the top, she helped him roll over onto his back on the catwalk. Gasping for breath, he was covered in sweat. She felt so bad for him. After a few moments she put a hand out to help him to his feet. Abruptly the doorknob to the reception room turned.

Mercy froze, still gripping Andrei's hand. Andrei turned and stared at the doorknob. The door creaked open a crack and she heard Thomas's voice.

"Wait, don't worry about it now. We can look over it tomorrow. It's getting late and you don't want to be caught in Kanta after dark."

"I suppose you're right." The door slid closed again and the doorknob turned back to normal. Mercy could breathe again.

Despite how much of a jerk Thomas could be, he was still protecting them. He risked much to keep them safe.

Though clearly worn out, Andrei let Mercy drag him to his feet. Neither of them wanted to be there anymore and, as quietly as they could, they ran along the catwalk toward the main tower.

Only when they were several grinders away did they slow down and finally talk.

"That was way too close for comfort." Andrei tried to catch his breath.

"Right?" She smiled, stopping for a moment so he could have a break.

Leaning against the railing, Andrei said, "And by the way, I love you, but I'm never crawling down into one of those grinders again. My arms feel like jelly."

She leaned in close and kissed his cheek. His skin was clammy and it wasn't a very good kiss, but she couldn't help it. Even if snow was beginning to fall again, she felt full of warmth. He actually loved her despite everything she had done.

Taking hold of his hand, she led the way to the kitchen, never wanting to let go again.

11

THE WOLF'S DEN

ANDREI ALWAYS HAD an appetite and having seen one of his transformations first hand, Mercy didn't blame him. The cook came each morning to prepare food for the day and only returned late in the evening to clean up. They were a mystery to Mercy. She couldn't fathom why anyone would agree to such a cryptic schedule in such a notoriously bizarre place, but she suspected Thomas had paid them enough to keep quiet about what they saw at the mill and look the other way when needed.

More than once she wondered if the cook had seen Mitchell's body at the foot of the stairs the night he died. If they had and hadn't said anything to anyone, that was almost more disturbing.

Long shadows fell across the wooden countertops and the tile flooring. The icebox was full of food each day, leftovers were available whenever she wanted, and fresh water was available to scoop out of buckets in the corner. She suspected even that was brought fresh from a local well each day, but couldn't be certain.

With a happy sigh, Andrei leaned back in his seat, having finished off two legs of fowl and a big bowl of rabbit stew. "Ahh, that feels better."

"You almost cleaned this place out," she said. With a grin, she pushed her own soup bowl back. "I guess you exert a lot of energy each night so it makes sense."

He gave her a pointed look. "I know you've been observing me for months now, but you don't have to talk about me as a specimen."

She winced. "Sorry, I don't mean to do that."

He rubbed at his chin. "You don't mean to do that when I can hear you, or you really don't mean to do that?"

She glared at him and got to her feet. "You know, you'll think differently if this compound I made actually is a cure. Maybe then you'll appreciate how observant I've been."

Andrei gave an awkward laugh. "Look, it was a joke. Don't get so bent out of shape." Despite his words, he stared down at his empty plate instead of looking at her. He might laugh to cover it up, but Mercy suspected there was more truth to his words than he let on.

She honestly didn't mean to analyze him all the time, but she had been studying him for so long she couldn't help herself. Andrei probably didn't want to hear it, but she knew his eating habits and sleeping routine better than he did.

Clacking the dirty dishes into the sink, she asked,

"Can you help and light the oil lamps? It's getting dark in here."

Without waiting for an answer, she carried a second pile of dishes to the sink and began scrubbing them.

"Sure," Andrei muttered. Then he went over and lit the two oil lamps, casting golden light into the darkening room.

She had only gotten halfway through the dishes when he came over and leaned against the metal drying rack. She could feel his eyes on her while she worked. Finally she dropped a fork into the metal sink with a loud clang and they both jumped. Soapy water flew up out of the sink and splashed both of them in the face. The room went silent for a second. They exchanged a nervous look, then Andrei started giggling.

"You have a glob of soap on your eyebrow!" He sputtered.

Mercy reached up and pulled the soap off, laughing at the splatter she wiped off. Andrei's laughter was contagious. Before she knew it, they were sitting on the tile floor, unable to stop laughing.

He put an arm around her shoulders and she pulled the towel down to dry her face, then tossed it into his face. That set them off all over again. He balled the towel up and flung it across the room. A comfortable silence filled the space between them and Mercy was relieved the tension was gone.

Leaning her head on Andrei's shoulder, she said, "I'm sorry I'm so weird, and I'm sorry I make you uncomfortable."

"If anyone is weird here, it's me."

Mercy pulled back. "You actually seem pretty normal to me. Except for when…" She trailed off, her gaze flitting across the room to the golden light from the oil lamps. "Oh no," she whispered.

"What's wrong?"

They no longer had long streaks of sunlight spilling across the kitchen tables. It was long past dusk and the sky was a dark gray. Mercy untangled herself and climbed to her feet. "Come on, we have to hurry!"

He must have thought she was joking at first because his smile faded to confusion. "What? You have a meeting with Thomas or something?"

"No!" She pulled on his hand, dragging him to his feet. "It's almost dark!"

His confusion turned to shock, then guilt, and finally melted to horror. "No…Already? I thought I had more time!"

"Winter days are so short," she cried.

They ran out of the kitchen and hurried down the stairs. Andrei was talking so fast she almost couldn't make out what he said.

"I am so sorry, Mercy! I am so, so sorry. I didn't even notice, and I'm the one that lit the damn oil lamps. I'm so stupid. I can't believe I did that! Last time this happened, it took Thomas *and* Leyda to get me into the cage, and I don't know where they are right now."

"It's okay," she breathed. "We both messed up, not just you."

Reaching the bottom floor, Mercy skidded to a halt. The door to the laboratory was shut and bolted. Why?

Who had done that? Had Leyda or Thomas closed up and forgot to check the cages?

Andrei didn't miss a beat, he ran over and began pulling down the large metal bars, but he was clutching his side at the same time, hunching forward as though it hurt to stand up straight.

Mercy licked her lips when she saw the first bar was pulled back. Only two more. Andrei leaned against the wall to catch his breath. He was in no condition for this.

"Who closed it?" she asked. "Why?"

"I don't know, but they're stronger than me." He gave an exhausted sigh. With a growl he went after the second bar, but this one was harder. As strong as he was, the transformation was coming on and he was running out of steam. He never got to pull the second one back.

Andrei bent over and clutched his belly, screaming in pain as his bones began to crack and reshape. Mercy put a hand to her mouth. She took a step back, trying to figure out what to do. There were no werewolf cages out here, only in the lab. A cage or two was in the reception chamber where werewolves were brought in, but she couldn't run back there in time. She could run up to her room and close the door, but that was a childish instinct. He could find her easily and that door was merely wood. If she raced up the stairs he would see her as prey and either pounce her before she got to the top or catch her scent and hunt her. Neither was a good option.

Blood pooled at Andrei's feet as his back tore open, his hips realigned, and his spine reformed. His jaw jutted forward as his fangs pierced through, and his warm, caramel eyes turned to the dangerous amber color.

Mercy thought back to her countless nights watching him transform. She stood her ground, took notes, which kept her from getting scared or fleeing in terror. During those frightening nights, she stayed a constant, calm presence for him. He didn't bite at her anymore or growl at her presence, he tolerated her, even when she took samples from him. If she tried to run away, she would be like any other prey animal and be run down.

But perhaps, if she treated this like any other night and stayed calm and confident, she might convince him to calm down. Maybe he would even go to sleep like he normally did after an hour or so.

The challenge would be to remain calm and confident while the werewolf had full range of the entire mill.

Andrei's panting slowed and he looked around in confusion. That was a good sign. At least he wasn't trying to bite her head off first thing.

"Hey, you're fine," she said in a calm voice, gesturing to the bloody mess at his feet. He whimpered at her—was he really scared?—before leaning down to lap at the blood. His eyes darted around, clearly nervous about the unfamiliar surroundings. He was smart as a werewolf, that had been one of the many observations she had made. They were far smarter than most hunters liked to admit.

Mercy avoided looking at him as she went over to sit with her back against the wall facing the stairwell. Andrei stopped lapping up the blood, so she knew he was watching her. When she settled on the floor, she calmly smoothed out her pants and leaned back, hopefully looking more like she was getting ready to have a picnic instead of preventing the man she loved from eating her.

When she started humming, he finally returned to lapping at the blood. She stole a glance at him. He wasn't looking at her, which was good. It meant he trusted her. She allowed herself to breathe a little easier, at least until he got curious.

She shouldn't have let Andrei gorge himself in the kitchen earlier because he clearly wasn't hungry. A full werewolf was a curious werewolf.

He paced around the entire rotunda with paws as big as her entire head. She tried not to let the clicking of his black claws on the metal floor make her panic, but her hands shook despite her efforts to keep them still. Then he started sniffing around the base of the stairs, even daring to put a paw on the first step.

"No," she warned in a voice that was firm but warm.

Amber eyes turned to her and Mercy felt like her heart wanted to beat out of her chest.

"No, you're not going upstairs. You're staying down here with me."

He gave a deep, guttural growl and Mercy felt her stomach do a somersault. His amber eyes fixed on her and Mercy couldn't tell if he was preparing to lunge or not.

She patted a spot on the floor beside her and then linked her hands together, trying to look like she was patiently waiting for him to join her, but also tried not to show her hands were shaking.

The werewolf glanced to the floor then locked eyes with her. Every time he stared at her like that, her stomach fluttered and she broke out in a sweat. Her father was right about one thing: the reaction to a werewolf's gaze was completely instinctual. She had very little control over it.

Andrei turned and put his paw back on the staircase. He was testing boundaries.

"I said no!" she demanded.

The werewolf turned and snapped his jaws at her. Mercy swallowed down the yelp at the back of her throat. She had made him angry, but he still hadn't come over to bite her throat out, so that had to be a good sign.

"Quit causing trouble and come lay down beside me." She patted the floor again and the werewolf snarled. But to her surprise, he padded over and slowly laid down beside her.

Mercy wanted to hug him. She wished she had her notebook with her to write all this down, but she didn't. She would have to be content with what she had: a fully transformed werewolf not on any drugs curled up beside her and fairly harmless—at least for the moment. If she kept yelling at him, that tenuous bond would be tested. Regardless of the authority in her voice, this was the wolf's den not hers.

"Thank you," she whispered but Andrei did not respond. He sniffed the air, bit at his fur in places, and looked around the room. At one point he belched.

She took back what she thought earlier, maybe it was best Andrei had filled up in the kitchen first.

"See, this isn't bad, is it?" She reached over and put a hand on his back, cautious and ready to pull back at the first sign of trouble. He didn't seem to care at all. In fact he propped his big paws out and started panting. If this kept up, he might be asleep soon.

Mercy allowed herself to smile. As much as Andrei hated her logging all of his daily habits, if she hadn't taken notes and samples on his transformation every night, she wouldn't be alive.

Then the werewolf shifted. A cold breeze alerted her to a change in the air. His entire body grew tense and he looked up at the top of the stairwell. His claws scraped across the metal floor. Was it the cook? Surely they wouldn't drop in so early in the evening.

"Shh, it's okay," she cooed. "Don't worry about them, you're fine and comfortable down here."

The hair on his back bristled and he uttered a deep warning growl. Mercy felt her insides quake at the sound, especially being so near to him. On instinct, she removed her hand from his back.

"Don't worry, you're fine. Nobody will hurt you," she whispered, but her voice betrayed her nerves.

Upstairs a door was flung open, footsteps on metal echoed down the stairwell. "Mercy? Why do I smell werewolf blood. Mercy!"

It was Leyda. Mercy shut her eyes and listened as she stormed around in her room upstairs. She wished she could call up to her, tell her to close up the tower and bunker down for the night while she took care of

Andrei. If she did, she knew the werewolf would pounce up those stairs in a flash.

The door slammed and she jumped.

"Thomas, get over here. Something has happened to one of the werewolves and Mercy is missing."

Andrei got to his feet, emitting a deep growl. Mercy stood up beside him, whispering reassurances to him, but nothing worked. He was entirely focused on Thomas and Leyda who spoke in low voices upstairs.

Of all the people in the mill, they were probably the worst ones to be here. The werewolf knew them. They were the ones who locked him in his cage when he started transforming the night they brought him to the mill. For all the werewolf knew, he had never left that cage. And now his captors were barking orders, clearly agitated, and completely unaware of Andrei's presence. It was a perfect time to pounce.

If, or rather when, he did pounce, what then? Mercy thought of Leyda's ferocity in fighting Mitchell that night. She was strong, but not as strong as a fully transformed werewolf. Either she or Andrei would win, and in the process someone could die. If Thomas saw a werewolf attacking Leyda, his first response would be to kill them. Hadn't that been Mercy's response when she saw Henry eating the officer that night? They didn't know this was Andrei. They didn't know him like she did, but if it meant life or death, Andrei would lose.

The werewolf crept to the stairwell, his claws no longer clicking on the metal. He was in full predator mode. Up above she heard footsteps on the metal staircase.

If Mercy didn't act now, she would never get another chance. She reached into her pockets and pulled out the compound and the darts. She flipped the lid up on the vial and dipped the dart in to soak just as she had for most of her life. She counted in her head, letting the liquid soak in. She had no idea how much Andrei needed or how much would be toxic. With practiced precision from making darts for her father for years, she replaced the lid on the vial and slipped it back into her pocket.

Up above Leyda and Thomas had reached the level with the kitchen. She couldn't hear what they were saying, but the tones of their voices revealed they were worried. Andrei crept up a couple more steps, unnervingly silent on the normally loud and rickety staircase.

Mercy clutched the dart in her hand and ran. She had one chance. It felt like the werewolf trap she performed ages ago with her father. If she made a single mistake or delayed at all, it could mean not only her life, but also the lives of Thomas, Leyda, and poor Andrei.

Andrei's werewolf form was so large he couldn't turn around easily on the stairwell as Mercy ran to him. She jammed the dart into his hide and he yelped. The look of betrayal in the werewolf's gaze hurt more than she expected, but she didn't stop. She rushed back to the opposite wall. Studying Andrei, she pulled out another dart to soak just in case. The werewolf was shocked and furious. He backed down the stairs and approached her with malice in his eyes. Whatever trust she had gained with him was now gone.

One of his back legs near the injection suddenly

didn't work right and he dragged it behind him as he approached. He wasn't going to let that slow him down. His amber eyes darkened to their dangerous ruby color.

"I'm sorry," Mercy whispered. "I had to. It was the only choice."

Andrei's other back foot went limp and then his hindquarters fell to the ground. He blinked in surprise and grunted in annoyance.

Leyda came into view on the staircase landing, followed by Thomas.

Mercy held a hand out to them, never removing her gaze from Andrei. "Stop, don't come down here!"

They froze at her command and Mercy was grateful. Andrei drooled thick saliva onto the floor as he dug his claws into the metal, dragging himself closer, so intent on his prey, so determined to take revenge for the betrayal. He was so smart, he understood that betrayal, she realized. How could that even be?

Mercy flattened herself against the wall, realizing too late that she had trapped herself. She also mentally kicked herself for how little she knew about her own compound. Would it bring him down? Would he be paralyzed for life? For all the praise Andrei showered on her, when it came down to it, she was a novice, an apprentice, no expert or wizard with chemicals. She had no idea what she had just given him. That was somehow more horrible to face than the snarling, drooling were-wolf before her.

"Shh, it's okay. You'll be alright," she lied.

He bared his fangs, his red eyes gleaming with rage. Even as one of his front paws went limp, she still saw the fury within him. He toppled to the ground, but still he fought the drug, fought it pulling him down. He lifted his head up and tried to snap at her. She felt the heat of his breath and smelled the brimstone of his saliva as the teeth closed mere inches from her face. Mercy turned her head to the side, trying to put as much distance as possible between herself and those jaws.

Finally Andrei collapsed completely, giving a sad whimper, no longer able to keep his head up. Fear filled his eyes as they slid closed. He whimpered once more before falling silent, his breathing deep and labored.

Mercy rested her head against the wall, trying to breathe. Yes, her experimental drug had stopped him, but what exactly had it done to him?

12

———

HOPE

AS SOON AS Andrei hit the floor, Leyda and Thomas hurried down the rest of the stairs. Mercy heard their footsteps echo on the metal steps, a part of her still frightened to look away from Andrei's hulking sleeping form before her.

Mercy closed her eyes and put a hand to her chest, trying to calm down and stop the rush of adrenaline that left her body shaking. Andrei took in slow, ragged breaths in front of her. He looked so relaxed when he was asleep compared to when he was awake. He looked calm, almost at peace. She had to hope that her drug would help him, not kill him. She had to hope she hadn't accidentally overdosed him or caused some permanent damage, that she would get to see him again and hear his voice. There was no other choice but to hope.

A warm arm wrapped around her shoulders and directed her away from the werewolf's jaws. Mercy was still shaking and trying to make sense of everything when Thomas pulled her into a tight hug.

"I can't believe you were down here with them alone. Please don't risk your life like that again. I don't want to lose you, Mercy." His voice trembled and it took her a moment to realize what was happening.

Tears streaked down her cheeks as he held her. Thomas would never be her father, but in that moment, he felt like it. Mercy hugged him back, grateful for his presence and his warmth, even if he was a broken, disturbed person. She tried to speak, but her voice wouldn't let her yet, so instead she hugged him back in silence.

"I promised your father." He stopped to clear his throat. "I promised him I wouldn't let harm come to you under this roof. Please don't turn me into a liar."

She shook her head, hoping he understood what she meant. Hoping he knew that wasn't her intention.

Leyda crouched down beside Andrei, poking and prodding at him in confusion. "Who is this? And what did you give them?" She leaned down and sniffed at his fur. "They smell strange. It wasn't Liquid Lead, was it?"

Mercy shook her head again and finally forced herself to speak. "It's Andrei. We lost track of time. We had an argument and I couldn't—" Her voice broke and she dipped her head. "It wasn't his fault, it was mine. I shouldn't have distracted him."

Thomas gave her another squeeze. It felt good to know that he did care for her, even if it was in his own bizarre way.

"Mercy, what did you dose him with?" he asked with far more warmth than Leyda. "I need to know, so I can see if we need to move him down to the laboratory or have him moved out front."

Out front. That's where they put werewolves who died. Out to the streets to be picked up by the morning rounds. They could be buried or burned, depending on how the body collectors felt that day and the state of the weather. That had been Henry's fate. Her chest tightened. It could be Andrei's. She swallowed down the panic that threatened to overwhelm her.

"It's a mixture I made. I have no idea if he's been overdosed because I've never used it before."

Thomas gently pulled away to look into her eyes, fear mingling with surprise in his eyes. "You made it?"

She nodded. "Andrei helped me read through your notes and study your reference books. I've been working on it for months. I know it reacts with werewolf anatomy…blood, tissue, saliva…but I have no idea what it does on a larger level."

Thomas and Leyda exchanged a look.

She glanced between them, fearful of their disappointment, just like her father's disappointment. She couldn't bear to see either of them upset with her over something she had been so proud of, over probably the best thing she had ever done. If it killed Andrei, she wouldn't want to see it again.

"It makes them no longer affected by silver, at least in samples. So I'm not sure what that means for the werewolf."

"Mercy…" Thomas muttered with a voice filled

with fear. "You're telling me you made him immune to silver?"

Leyda backed away from Andrei and drew closer to them. "Perhaps we should be having this conversation elsewhere, Thomas."

"Yes, I agree," he muttered and began directing Mercy toward the stairs. But before they could reach them, Andrei let out a howl of pain.

All three of them jumped and turned to see Andrei writhing and crying out on the ground. He clawed at the metal, leaving long white streaks behind. He rolled, howling and screaming, into the stairwell. His shrieks hurt Mercy's ears and she winced with each cry.

"What's wrong with him?" she asked, but Thomas looked just as bewildered.

Finally Andrei curled inward, clutching at his stomach and hacking out blood onto the floor. It was tinged with black and Mercy suddenly thought of the black taint the silver caused in the tiny vial of werewolf blood she had demonstrated to Andrei earlier. Her stomach sank.

"I've poisoned him!" She cried, running toward him but unable to get too close. "Andrei, can you hear me at all? I am so sorry. I didn't mean to hurt you."

She placed her hands on his side, but instead of fur and muscle, she felt something shifting beneath the surface. His side rippled as muscle and bone moved underneath and she yanked her hands back in alarm.

"Oh no," she whispered. He howled again as his back ripped open and his spine snapped.

"He's not poisoned," Thomas said, stepping closer. "He's transforming."

Leyda grabbed Mercy's arm and dragged her back to the base of the steps. "It looks like he's transforming, but into what exactly? We have no idea what the girl's poison is doing to him."

Mercy felt her heart break at her words. What if she was right, what if Mercy had accidentally poisoned him, or turned him into something worse? He could die right here in front of them, and there was nothing she could do to stop it. She was an amateur, a novice. What kind of a fool did she think she was playing with chemicals and thinking she could make something from it?

She remembered how Henry transformed back into a human after she shot him, was this the same thing? A brief cold pit formed in her heart. It was a familiar feeling, one she hadn't felt in a while. The last time she felt it was when she lost her father. No, she couldn't let that happen again. She couldn't bear to lose someone else she cared about. She couldn't let that coldness overcome her again.

Andrei's limbs reformed, his face flattened inward, and his fur retracted. Finally what lay on the cold metal floor was no longer a ferocious werewolf, but Andrei again, naked and covered in sweat. He turned onto his side, his head flopping to the metal floor, his eyes wide with shock as he took in the room.

"Mercy?" He called in a hoarse voice, his eyes were taking longer to transform. They were still shifting from wolf to human. "Oh please don't tell me I hurt you.

Please tell me you're still alive." He couldn't see her yet, Mercy realized, and she nearly sobbed in response.

Leyda's jaw dropped and Thomas barked a laugh. Mercy broke free from Leyda's grip, taking advantage of her distraction, and ran over to Andrei's side. She wrapped her fur coat over him and helped him sit up.

"I'm fine!" She kissed him, ignoring Thomas's laughter from behind. Slowly the amber of his eyes shifted back to his warm caramel color again and she kissed him again. "You changed back. You're human and it's night still for hours yet."

"What?" He blinked as Mercy hugged him. "Wait, it's still night? But how?"

Thomas removed his cape and wrapped it over Andrei's shoulders. "It seems like Mercy has found the cure to lycanthropy."

"Mercy?" Andrei grinned and all the terror she'd endured the last hour was worth it to see his beautiful smile again. "Wait, your compound actually worked?" He hugged her so hard she couldn't breathe for a moment. "You're brilliant!"

"You made a cure?" Leyda's voice was hoarse. "That smart-mouthed child we rescued from the woods made a cure for lycanthropy?"

A vise-like grip took hold of Mercy's bicep and yanked her away from Andrei. Next she knew she stared into the furious eyes of Leyda.

"Ow, let go! That hurts!"

"Do you have more? Give it to me! Give me the damn cure, girl." Leyda shook her. Mercy couldn't pry her fingers off, but the pain was terrible. Leyda only squeezed tighter. "Give it to me!"

Thomas put a hand on Leyda's shoulder, trying to pull her away. "Leyda, please, there are more tests to be done before we know if this is a true cure. Let go of her!"

"Back off, Thomas!" She snarled and bared her teeth at him. "I have lived as this monster you've turned me into for far too long. I lost my family looking like this, the love of my life! You will not make me live a day longer like this!" With her free hand she grabbed Thomas and flung him away, easily taking him off his feet, and sent him skidding across the floor where he knocked into the wall.

"No!" Mercy cried.

"Leyda, stop! She said you're hurting her," Andrei demanded, scrambling to his feet. "Let go of her already!"

"Not until she gives me the same cure you got, lover-boy. You don't know the hell I've been through!"

Mercy was afraid Leyda might actually break her arm. She couldn't reach the vial even if she wanted to with Leyda holding her so tight. Her arm throbbed in protest and she couldn't feel her fingers any longer.

Andrei swept his arm back and suddenly it wasn't a human arm, but a far longer one, covered in fur, with a paw the size of Mercy's skull. Blood dripped down his elbow and long black claws shot out of his bloody fingertips. With a snarl, he raked his claws across Leyda's side.

Crying out, Leyda backed away clutching at her

wound and finally releasing her hold. Mercy took shaky steps back, cradling her arm, feeling the blood rush into it again. Andrei was at her side in an instant, his werewolf arm far longer than his human one. He put his good arm around her and pulled her backward and away from Leyda.

"Are you okay?" he asked. "Is it broken?"

"I don't think so," Mercy muttered.

Thomas got to his feet with a groan. Leyda stared at Andrei in bewilderment. His werewolf arm was suddenly back to being human again. Other than the bloody trails down his arm and across the floor, there was no evidence that it had even changed.

"It isn't a cure," Leyda whispered, her voice shrill with shock and anguish. "Thomas, it isn't a cure at all. It's something else."

Thomas rubbed at the back of his neck, and wrapped an arm around Leyda's shoulders. "Yes, it is something else entirely," he whispered. "I believe Mercy has discovered something that just might be better than a werewolf cure."

Leyda stumbled over her words, barely able to look her in the eye. "Mercy, I'm sorry. I—I don't know why I did that, I just…I'm tired, Thomas. I'm tired of being this." She buried her face into her hands, her partially transformed muzzle poking out between her fingers. "I'm so tired of being a monster!"

"Shh, I know," Thomas whispered. "It's alright. I'm sure Mercy doesn't take it personally." He gave Mercy an apologetic expression.

Mercy's arm still throbbed, but she couldn't help but

feel sorry for Leyda, stuck somewhere between a were-wolf and a human, without the advantage that Andrei now had. In all honesty, Mercy wasn't sure if the compound would work on her or leave her stuck permanently in the half-transformed state she hated.

"I thought it was a real cure!" Leyda wailed, leaning against Thomas.

"I'm sorry I got your hopes up," Mercy said, walking over to her and putting a hand on her arm.

Leyda turned to her, her head bowed. "I am sorry I hurt you, Mercy. Sometimes I can't control myself. I don't know why."

"Hey, I'm the one that tried to eat everybody." Andrei gave an awkward laugh. "Sure, this isn't a cure, but it's a start. I'm, um, sorry about the claws by the way. I know how those can smart."

Leyda gave a defeated shrug.

"Imagine what the werewolf pack will think of this," Mercy said with a gleam in her eye. "Imagine what people will think when they realize werewolves are walking among them, looking like them."

Thomas gave a wicked laugh. "Oh yes, soon the woods will be bereft of werewolves to hunt. Ahh, this is going to completely change business in Kanta. And as usual, I'll be on the cutting edge of progress with my mechanical grinders." His lazy eye drifted to her.

Mercy guessed he would try to claim it was his idea from the start, not that she would let him. She wasn't about to let him forget that his last great idea led to werewolves having their arms ripped off and forcing them into grueling manual labor for the rest of their days. Enough truths in Kanta were forgotten, and she wouldn't let this one pass.

"Just remember that we did this together, Andrei and I. If he wasn't a willing specimen for me, I never would have made so much progress."

Andrei nudged her. "You saying I'm a good test subject?"

"Don't let it go to your head." She rolled her eyes.

"Well, as a prized test subject, I have a few demands to make of this establishment."

Mercy grinned. "Oh?"

"Oh yeah. First up, I want to find some real clothes. My old ones are all shredded…again. Then food. I'm starving."

Mercy stifled a laugh.

"After that." He glanced to Mercy. "I guess I'll be a living petri dish for you for a while, is that right? I mean, now that you're a real scientist and all that."

"Indeed!" Thomas beamed. "She's made more progress in months then I have in ages. I think she deserves her own office space down in the laboratory too. That is, if she's amiable with that idea."

Mercy felt her cheeks get hot. Andrei gave her a dorky grin, Thomas was praising her skills, talking about giving her an office of all things. Even Leyda looked at her with maybe even a small amount of admiration. Mostly she felt hope, something she hadn't felt or known in such a very long time. She hoped she could live up to their expectations. Disappointment was what she feared the most.

"That would definitely help. Thank you, Thomas.

The work has only begun if I plan to find a full cure one day."

Thomas nodded and glanced to Leyda. "And maybe you can help me clean up my scientific mistakes I've made along the way." There was a pleading in his voice that pulled at her heart.

"I don't think she could fix your mistakes if she had years to do it," Leyda muttered and Thomas chuckled. "Be practical, Thomas. I know that's hard for you."

Mercy walked over to Leyda and took her hand, "I can't promise anything, you know that. I'm too new at this. But I can try. I can promise you that."

Leyda looked like she might cry again, but instead she merely nodded. "Thank you." She took a deep breath. "Even your failures give me hope."

Mercy took a deep breath. She never thought she would go from werewolf hunter apprentice, to mill assistant, to researcher and chemist in her life, but here she was. As proud as she felt of her accomplishments, and of Andrei's progress, she knew she had much left to do. People like Leyda, the werewolves in the lab, the werewolves from the grinders, and the pack members in the woods—all of them needed her help. There was a lot of work to do and it relied on more than just her chemical experiments.

Somehow she would find a way to help them. She had to. They needed her. She had found a way to continue her father's goal of cleaning out the wolves of Kanta, but in a far better, more humane way. And Kanta was merely the beginning.

She took Andrei's hand in hers and prepared for the next experiment. It would surely be the first of many.

To be continued in Book 3:
The Hunters of Kanta

AFTERWORD

Welcome to the path that Mercy chose for her future, one filled with chemicals, Bunsen burners, and werewolf blood. It certainly isn't the path I expected when I first wrote her story in The She-Wolf of Kanta, but this is what she chose and I couldn't be happier. I have an excuse to share my love of science and my love of werewolves, what could be better? Mercy is a transformative character, one who changes so much in this series, and I'm so happy to share her story.

A big thank you goes out to all the readers who wanted to read more of Mercy's story after getting a taste of this world in The She-Wolf of Kanta. Thank you for telling me that you wanted more, and thank you for sharing your love for her character and her story. This wouldn't have been written without your feedback!

The Wolves of Kanta series continues in Book 3: The Hunters of Kanta. I can't wait to share the characters and the places we get to explore, not to mention the terrors that await her and Andrei.

Thank you so much for your support, and I hope to see you back for book 3!

Marlena
October 24, 2021

ALSO BY MARLENA FRANK

The Stolen Series

Young adult, portal fantasy, faeries

Stolen

Broken

Chosen

The Wolves of Kanta Series

Young adult, dark fantasy, steampunk, werewolves

The She-Wolf of Kanta

The Blood of Kanta

The Hunters of Kanta

The Fury of Kanta

The Howl of Kanta

Standalones

Young adult, horror, sci-fi, dystopian

The Seeking

Short stories, horror, dark fantasy

The Impostor and Other Dark Tales

Ocean horror, weird, short story

Undertow

Weird western, werewolves, vampires, short story
Night Feeders

Mystery, film noir, humor, short story
The Mysterious Disappearance of Charlene Kerringer

 **Join the Mailing List** 

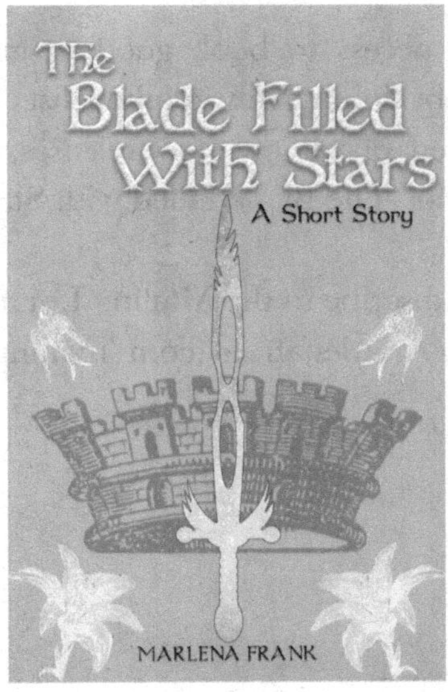

The Blade Filled with Stars

A kingdom is under siege from a familiar enemy. Families and friends are pitted against each other without reason. Slaughter is imminent while the winged Queen Khafil soars overhead. Desperate and terrified, Anna works with her sister, Lilah, to summon aid from their mother's ancient spell book.

Determined to save their people, the sisters

summon Death to help them, but Death is not easily swayed. Neither of the sisters are prepared for the consequences.

Want a peek behind the scenes?
Want to preview my books before they get released?

Get exclusive access to book goodies, giveaways, and cover reveals by joining my mailing list. Not only will you get notified of all my new releases, you'll get an exclusive copy of The Blade Filled with Stars.

Subscribe to the Mailing List at:
http://marlenafrank.com/mailinglist/

Support Me On

Ko-fi

Follow me on Ko-Fi for regular updates on my writing progress.

Monthly subscribers get access to sneak peeks at stories way before anyone else. They also get access to cover reveals, monthly shout-outs on social media, and thanked by name in the acknowledgements in my books.

http://ko-fi.com/MarlenaFrank

ACKNOWLEDGMENTS

Deciding to kick off a series from The She-Wolf of Kanta was a tough choice. I knew going in that it was going to take time and determination to make sure I did Mercy and the world justice. Once I found the story that needed to be told, I knew I needed to make this happen. It was a long journey to get here and I have a lot of people to thank.

Thank you to Lara, my fantastic editor, who was willing to take on the series on short notice when my previously lined up editor fell through. She made such a difference with this book and helped me to lean into the STEM themes that I shied away from initially. Sometimes it's hard for me to merge my scientific background with my creative works because I'm so used to keeping those two facets separated in my daily life. Thank you for helping me overcome that hurdle and for bringing this book to life.

A big thank you to my sister, Kelley, who once again kept me motivated to keep fleshing out the world and the characters. She always reminds me that it's okay to let my young adult work get a little spooky. She reminds me to lean into that if the story needs it.

Another big thanks to my parents who have always

fully supported my author life. My Mom gave me some wonderful pointers on where she thought the thematic heart of this world lay and that helped me shape Mercy's journey. My aunt Charmaine, my constant cheerleader, not only crows to her friends about how amazing She-Wolf is, but also encourages me to keep writing.

Thank you to Carla, who has stood beside me through thick and thin, for being a constant encouragement and cheerleader for all of my work. This series wouldn't exist without her. I appreciate every time she is willing to be a shoulder to lean on and an ear to listen. She is such an incredible author and I'm lucky to have her as a friend.

To Candace for checking in on me, being a sanity check, and for helping me with countless pitfalls—many of which I wouldn't know exist without her help. She is always there to help regardless of what question comes up in this indie author sea we are both sailing in. Her beautiful writing helped me work the courage up to flesh out Mercy and Andrei's relationship in this book. I don't think I'll ever be able to thank her enough for her support.

One of the constant supporters on my journey has been my Ko-Fi supporter, Donna. She has somehow waited patiently for years for this book to come out and I hope it lives up to her expectations. When I think of my readers, I think of her first because she is so supportive of my work and is always there to give words of encouragement.

Like Mercy, I too fear disappointment, and I'm grateful to each of these people for building me up when the writing waters get rough and turbulent. Thank you for being there for me, for supporting me, and for believing in me!

ABOUT THE AUTHOR

Marlena Frank is the author of books and novellas that span genres from young adult fantasy to horror. Her debut novel, Stolen Book 1 of the Stolen series, has hit the Amazon bestseller charts twice.

Marlena's short fiction has been included in notable anthologies such as Heroic Fantasy Quarterly, Not Your Average Monster Volume 2, and The Sirens Call issue #29.

Although she was born in Tennessee, Marlena has spent most of her life in Georgia. She lives with her sister and three spoiled cats. She is an affiliate member of the Atlanta Chapter of the Horror Writers Association and is also an avid member of the Atlanta cosplay community.

She is also an INFJ, a tea drinker, and a wildlife enthusiast.

Support her on Ko-Fi: ko-fi.com/MarlenaFrank